JOHN FRANKLIN BARDIN was born in Cincinnati in 1916. After a difficult childhood – including the loss of his mother through mental illness – he lived in Chicago and New York, where he was an executive in an advertising agency. He published ten novels and taught creative writing as well as advertising. Bardin died in the East Village on 9 July, 1981.

DEVIL TAKE THE
BLUE-TAIL FLY

John Franklin Bardin

First published in the UK in 1948 by Victor Gollancz

This edition published in Great Britain in 2001 by
Canongate Crime, an imprint of
Canongate Books Ltd, 14 High Street,
Edinburgh EH1 1TE

10 9 8 7 6 5 4 3 2 1

British Library Cataloguing-in-Publication Data
A catalogue record for this book is available
on request from the British Library

ISBN 1 84195 164 1

Typeset by Palimpsest Book Production Limited,
Polmont, Stirlingshire
Printed and bound by Omnia Books Ltd, Glasgow.

To
John C. Madden
WITH RESPECT AND
ADMIRATION

When I was young I used to wait,
On massa and give him his plate,
And pass the bottle when he got dry
And brush away the blue-tail fly.

Chorus:

Jimmy crack corn and I don't care,
Jimmy crack corn and I don't care,
Jimmy crack corn and I don't care.
My massa's gone away.

And when he'd ride in the afternoon,
I'd follow after with a hickory broom,
The pony being rather shy,
When bitten by a blue-tail fly.

Chorus

One day he ride round the farm,
The flies so numerous they did swarm,
One chanced to bite him on the thigh –
The devil take the blue-tail fly!

Chorus

The pony run, he jump, he pitch
He threw my massa in the ditch;
He died and the jury wondered why –
The verdict was the blue-tail fly!

Chorus

They lay him under a 'simmon tree
His epitaph is there to see –
'Beneath this stone I'm forced to lie –
Victim of the blue-tail fly!'

Chorus

AN AUTHENTIC NEGRO MINSTREL SONG
OF *circa* 1840

Today is the day, was her first waking thought – and she repeated it, charmed by the echoing syllables, the rise and fall of the cadence, saying the words aloud this time, playfully accenting one of them: 'Today is *the* day.' Ellen breathed deeply and stretched her arms upward towards the pale-green ceiling until her joints cracked and her tendons strained. The clear morning light washed the immaculate box of a room, splashed it with sun as a dasher splashes cream in a churn. Ellen laughed at the image, pleased with the ingenuity of her mind. Why, she hadn't ever really forgotten anything, had she? Only once in her life had she seen a churn, only once – during that month, the first month of their marriage, when Basil and she had stayed at that farm in Vermont – had she seen the thick yellow cream, the queer whitish butter that had tasted so marvellously rich, the frothy paddle. Oh, she was well again, there was no doubt about it, or she would not have thought of that. And it was so apt – the sun on the bland green walls did look like cream turning to butter, and she did feel happy. In fact, she felt as happy now as she had felt that month, that incredibly idyllic month, when Basil and she had first been married. Her mood and the sun and the butter, they were all the same; it was all of a piece. Ellen let her hands fall abruptly and, with a tremendously contented sigh, let her lungs empty out the huge breath she had been holding in, guarding jealously, as if in this way she could clasp the perfection of the moment to her. And, bounding and bouncing despite the stiffness of the springs and mattress, she threw back the covers and jumped out of bed. 'Today I am going home!'

Basil was coming for her. She would take his arm, a little gravely, a little self-consciously, and walk down the corridor with him. She would stand beside him while Martha – or would it be Mary? – unlocked the door, only this time she would not clutch his arm any tighter, her fingers would not tense against the rough tweed of his sleeve. For this time she would not have to stop at the door, she would not have to stand there, helpless, while Basil kissed her cheek, her brow, and then, with a caution he had not once known, her mouth. She would not have to smile and say something casual, something meaningless but cheery, to Martha – sometimes it had been Mary – while he walked rapidly past the door, down the hall, clattered on the iron, the fireproof, stairs. She would not have to turn around and walk back up the corridor to her room, just like the others, even with the monks' cloth hangings, the bound scores of Bach and Handel, Rameau and Couperin, Haydn and Mozart, in the bookcase that she had requested and Basil had brought her from town. Not today! No, never again would she sit by the window, her back turned so she would not see him walk down the flagstone path with Dr Danzer, the limp

2

volume of her favourite Bach spread open to the first page of the text, the black notes swarming before her eyes, her fingers arching in elaborate dumb-show as they practised the first trill, her mind on the beats, the leaning upon the upper note, the precise apperception of the stopping point – not a moment too soon, not a moment too late – and in her ears once more the sound, the slow dignity, of Anna Magdalena's sarabande, a delicate ornament for her melancholy.

'I am going home today!' She said it again, laughing under her breath, brushing her brisk blonde hair until it was vibrant and sparkled when touched. She dressed quickly, surely, not hesitating over what she was to wear, but choosing irrevocably the forest-green suit, the brown oxfords with sensible heels, the hat with the feather which she did not particularly like but which Basil had selected himself and brought to her so proudly. There had been no choice, of course, or rather she had done the choosing months ago, when she had first dared to look forward to this day. All except the hat, that is; she had decided on another hat – a mannish affair that suited her and the occasion better. But then Basil had brought this hat and she could not but wear it, since she would not hurt him for all the world. No, from now on Basil's happiness came first, was her *sine qua non*, for he deserved it. Where would she be without Basil? Who had looked after her, talked and reasoned with her when she was sickest, stood by without faltering? Basil. Who had come to see her every visiting day, even when he knew there was no use, that they would not let him see her, coming from the city by train to the town, from the town by crowded bus to the hospital? Basil. And then, the last time he had come – after they had told him – he had brought her the hat.

A silly hat, a frippery thing with a nonsensical feather, the kind women buy when they're in love and men buy when they go into a store and are embarrassed and say, finally, stammering, 'I want a hat.' And both times the betrayal is accompanied by the same sales-girl words, 'Madame will find it so chic!' – the same slurred speech, the same shamed groping for purse or billfold, the same flush when one thinks of the incident later and knows, whether one admits it or not, that one's been had. But, after all, what did it matter? What if the day did seem to require a more serious head-dress, a more sober hat? Hadn't Basil bought this silly thing, and wasn't that one fact worth more than any female prejudice? Oh, there was no question about that hat – she would wear it and love wearing it, for she loved Basil, and today she was going home with him. That was all that mattered, that was the wonderful fact.

After she had finished dressing, after she had made the stiff, high hospital bed for the last time, she looked at her watch, and saw that it was yet only a few minutes past six. Breakfast would not be until seven, the doctor would not see her before eight; even if Basil had taken the afternoon train yesterday, as he had promised he would, and stayed overnight at the town's one hotel, he could hardly be at the hospital before nine. She had three hours or more to pack her clothes, her books and scores, to say good-bye to Mary and Martha, to thank Dr Danzer for all he had done for her – three more hours, at least, of leave-taking. It would be a long time, now it seemed that it would never be over; but, then, would it be long enough? What are three hours in two years, especially when those hours are heavy with the burden of those years, when all the past time endured weighs on the present interval, makes each moment massive with meaning? From six to nine she would be aware of each instant in its passing, as it seemed to her she had known intimately every hour of the night and day of the two years that were ending. But – and she looked at the window, saw through it the green lawn and the curving flagstone walk, the elms that lined the high stone wall, the wrought-iron gate and the brick cube that was the gatekeeper's lodge – nine o'clock would come; although the intervening time would pass slowly, Basil would come, and she would take his arm, smile up at him, and then, finally and irrefutably, the years and the hours would be over.

She went to the bookcase and ran her hands over the narrow-backed, gilt-stamped volumes of her scores, her fingers arching and pointing, forming arpeggios, appoggiaturas and glissandos, feeling the firmness of the buckram, the softness of the vellum, aching for the last time for the hard, polished veracity of keys, imagining the bright, satisfying, metallic sound of a plucked string, hearing in her mind's ear the heart of the note, the vibration of a chord, the tinkling precision of a sweeping run, a trill. A few hilly miles on a lurching bus, Basil beside her holding her hand, the rush of a train drawn as by a magnet to the city, the frustration of a taxi's stops and starts, Basil close to her, enclosed in the small space with her, his ears annoyed like hers by the metronomic tick of the meter, and she would be going up the stone steps of their house, exchanging bows with Suky, the butler – his a lithe swoop, hers a dipping of her head, a shrugging of her shoulders – then she would be past Suky, running up the stairs to her study, pausing at the door to seek the rose walls, the soft overhead lighting, the long couch where she could stretch out when her back was tired, the bow window, but pausing only an instant before stepping confidently forward to her instrument, sitting on the bench and running her hands softly over the old wood of the lid, then lifting it back on itself to reveal the manuals, the rows of keys, bringing her hand down abruptly; but, as she felt the ivory surfaces give, drawing back, holding back, slightly, hearing the chord and its overtones as her foot pressed the pedal, the sharp cleanness of sound's heart surrounded by a cloud of overlapping tones, the essence of music that only with a harpsichord can one distil. That would be noon – noon at the latest; but it might be before, when she could play again. Her fingers would not obey her; she was reconciled to this – although she had tried to keep them supple throughout the years of her alienation by exercise and silent practice. She would know the scores – she knew them backwards and forwards, she had scanned them so many times – but she was sure that at first her fingers would stumble, her coordination would be poor, her attitude tense, her rhythm inconsistent. But she would be at the keyboard again, she could strike the plangent notes whenever she desired, pick out a melody, devise an ornamentation, and with the days that lay in the future would come long mornings and afternoons at her instrument, her fingers working at the keys bit by bit reassembling the knacks, learning again to translate the ideal sound she heard in her head into actual music. It would come, it would come – it would all be hers again. And, thinking this, she began to pick the volumes from the shelves, one and two at a time, and carried them to the suitcase that lay open on the bed, fitting them carefully inside, walking back and forth, quickly, quietly, happily.

When she had packed all her books and scores and

had closed the large suitcase, had tugged its heavy bulk off the bed and set it on the floor, she placed the two smaller travelling-cases on the room's two chairs and went to the closet to gather her few clothes. Two old dressing-gowns, a few dresses, several more pairs of oxfords and one pair of pumps that she had worn but once, on a day soon after she had first come to the hospital; had slipped and fallen in them, had had them taken away from her – they had not been returned for many months – along with her manicure scissors, her watch, her fountain-pen, her nailfile: all the little objects she had become used to, depended on, but which they had taken from her, saying, 'You won't need these now, will you?' and, of course, she had needed them – more than that, she had wanted them; but she had known that to protest would have been useless, that they had their routine, their methods, and that even Basil said that they knew best. Besides these shoes and dresses, the closet held her coat which she had used this winter for the first time to take long walks with Martha and Mary, her other hats, and that was all. She made three or four armfuls of them and dumped them into the two cases, straightening them with hurried pokes and deft pattings, taking much less care with them than she had with the volumes of scores, knowing that she would not wear them again, except, perhaps, around the house – the styles would be so different; she would need so many new things.

She emptied the drawer of the shiny, white metal cabinet where she had kept her stockings, her underclothing and other oddments, and put them all together in one bag, without looking at them, closed and latched it swiftly and decisively. Standing in the centre of the room, she looked around to see what she had forgotten, what remained that belonged to her and she wanted to keep – not that there had ever been much. The radio she had given to Mary months ago, since the only stations she had been able to get on it had played insufferable programmes, dramatic serials, jazz, commercials, the news; although once it had served her well – during the days when she had first begun to grow better, when she had been allowed to see Basil again and he had bought her the little set with its gaudy dial and varnished cabinet: days when it had been reassuring just to hear a voice in the room, a voice that belonged to a stranger, with a stranger's false warmth and affability, a voice that was without a doubt human, yet belonged to someone who did not know her, was not concerned with her, could not possibly have any designs on her. The pictures that she had asked Martha to clip from magazines and which she had taped to the wall, a line-drawing by Picasso, a four-colour version of one of Renoir's auburn-haired girls, a severe Mondrian diagram and one of Leonardo's drawings for a flying-machine, she had pulled off and torn up and thrown away the night before, knowing that no patient or nurse would want them – that they had had their purpose of reminding her of the order that still existed in the world and which she must emulate, but that now their function was no longer needed, she would soon be back in her own house, surrounded by the paintings Basil and she had bought together, and that these substitutes were better destroyed. There was nothing left but the monks'-cloth drapes at the windows, and she hesitated to pull them down; they would leave the room naked, make obvious its sterility, emphasize its restrictions. Although she knew she should not, that what came after was no concern of hers, she could not help thinking of its next occupant, could not help projecting upon this person the despair, the aloneness, the fear she had herself felt when she had come into this room for the first time, saw its green walls, its high bed, its lattice-guarded windows, knew that it was a locked box, a cell, a grave for the living. She remembered the nights she had lain awake, fighting off the sedative they had given her, watching the moonlight, shattered into glowing fragments by the criss-cross of the lattice, creep along the floor, the walls, the bed, menacing her. And she recalled the sharp shards of splintered sun that stabbed like daggers at her eyes on brilliant days. And she walked to the other chair, bent over the second travelling-case and slammed it shut, clicked its latches and turned the key in the lock, deciding that she would leave the drapes at the windows where they belonged.

Mary brought her breakfast a few minutes later, a familiar breakfast that she had eaten many times before: orange-juice, cold but tasting of the can from which it had been poured; oatmeal, thick and warm and gelatinous; two slices of whole wheat bread and a pat of bright yellow butter; coffee with a little bottle of cream and one packaged lump of sugar which she never used but which she still found on the saucer every time. Mary's face was as scrubbed and shining as ever – Ellen had a fancy that after she washed it she must rub it with a cloth until it shone like ten-cent store silverware – her iron-grey hair, neat as coils of wire, bulged at her cap, obtruding here and there, as it always had before. But this morning Ellen felt that the smile on the attendant's face was less automatic than usual, that the quick gestures of her hands showed a certain nervousness that might be attributed to enthusiasm, that Mary, like herself, was glad that Basil was coming, that she was going home.

9

'Dr Danzer will be a little late this morning, Mrs Purcell,' Mary said, and then, without pausing, 'where shall I put the tray – here, on the table?'

Ellen came across the room, nodding her head, plucking the glass of orange-juice from the tray before the attendant could set it down, gulping the cold stuff to escape the tang she did not like.

'I'm going home today, Mary,' she said, knowing it was superfluous, but wanting to say the words aloud again just to hear their wonderful sound, as she might hum a tune of Mozart over and over to herself because to hear it made her happy.

The nurse nodded briskly, but the lines about her eyes crinkled, and Ellen could see that she was relaxed, that for once, at least, Mary stood before her, if not as a friend, as a neutral person. 'We are going to miss you, Mrs Purcell,' she said, and as she said this she really smiled. 'You are our favourite patient, you know.'

Ellen tried the oatmeal with her spoon, looked down at the tray to keep the attendant from seeing how pleased she was to hear her say that. 'Am I?' she said, not that she doubted it, but, childishly, to coax more praise. 'I did not know.'

'That's what Dr Danzer says.'

Ellen let the spoon drop on the plate with a clatter and turned around to see who had spoken. It was Martha, who stood in the doorway – she was smiling, too; but, then, Martha always smiled.

The two attendants were very different types: Martha, tall, young and blonde, with a lovely face which she made-up carefully and the kind of long-limbed grace to her movements that is more common to a model or an actress than an attendant; Mary, short and heavy-set, but firmly-fleshed, older than Martha but not yet old, quick and machine-like in her habits, grave and ever-watchful. Still, in them, it was not their differences that were remarkable, but their similarities. They seemed always to be present, always alert, always wary – even when Ellen had not seen them, she had known that they were lurking somewhere. They were always looking at you when they were with you, their eyes were upon you no matter what they were doing, they kept you under surveillance. Ellen had at one time resented their vigilance and had complained bitterly to herself about it. She had felt isolated by it as a prisoner under armed guard must feel isolated from the rest of humanity. Even this morning, when she knew that there was no reason for them to regard her in any way other than a friendly one, she looked for indications of their wariness, was relieved to find it absent, but kept seeking it again, as if expecting it to return.

Martha had come into the room and had walked over to the table. If she would only turn her back to me! Ellen thought, then I would be sure that she means what she says. She looked down at her plate again and picked up her spoon, this time actually scooping some of the oatmeal into her mouth, swallowing the warm, gluey mess. Martha was still talking, her voice casual and pleasant, confiding, 'Yes, Dr Danzer was telling us just the other day that you are his *triumph*. That he had never had a patient who responded to treatment as well as you – who effected such a complete *adjustment*.' The second attendant had an emphatic manner of speaking that Ellen had often found annoying. She accented words not because of their position in the phrase, the clause, the sentence, as Ellen liked to do herself, but to underscore their meaning. Martha talked to one as she might to a child. Even when she did not repeat what she said, the effect of her words was that of repetition, of deliberation, of instruction. And beneath this emphasis Ellen detected the ring of authority, the hint of command.

She looked up from her food at both of them, tall and short, standing beside her. 'It's kind of you to say that,' she said. 'But how could anyone keep from getting well with such good care?' She had thought this out and sensed that this was what she should say: it was a statement that showed poise and equanimity and assurance – all the qualities that once she had not had. But, in some subtle fashion, it was also a lie, an untruth that she found troublesome. Mary and Martha, she liked them well enough, and they had never been unkind to her – but it was also true that she was glad that she was never going to see them again; that their personalities, their watchfulness, formed as much a part of the life she was escaping as the lattice-work on the window.

'Some don't—' said Mary, and then shut her mouth on the rest that she had been about to say. And, as a member of a team helps a mate to recover a fumble, Martha stepped into the gap of silence that followed, saying:

'Dr Danzer tells us that you are going to take up your music again – that you are going to play in concert. Will you send us tickets to your first recital?'

'I shall – I promise,' Ellen said, eating several spoonsful of the oatmeal; 'the very first concert I give. But I warn you that you may not like it – my fingers are so stiff. I'm afraid I may have lost the knack.' And while she talked she was thinking. What had Mary meant by 'some don't—'? Had she meant that some don't recover completely ever? Of course, this was true, and she knew it. Or had the older nurse started to say, and then stopped because of tact, that some seemed to recover, but relapsed, that some did not stay adjusted, that the old fears returned and with them the old malady?

On impulse, with false bravery, more to test herself and the strength of her will than out of any inner necessity, Ellen said, 'Martha, now, before I leave' – she stopped and laughed to make it like a joke – 'I want you to do me a favour. I want you to turn your back on me, I want both of you to turn your backs on me – both you, Martha, and you, Mary – and keep them turned for more than a minute!'

Martha smiled and said nothing. Mary did not smile. They both looked at her in silence, not for long, although it seemed long to her, while she took another spoonful of the oatmeal. She lowered her eyes, thinking that they might want to look at each other, to gauge the other's thoughts to see if they both thought it wise. But as soon as she looked down, she forced herself to look up again – if they had regarded each other, it had been only a flick of a glance, yet she felt that somehow they had managed it, for Martha was smiling again. But then, Martha always smiled.

'Why, of course, if you want,' said Mary. 'But I don't see why?' And then, after having said she would, she did not, and neither did Martha. But they both stood there looking at her, awaiting an explanation, smiling. And Ellen knew that once more she would have to explain.

'It's silly of me, I know,' she said, 'but all the time I've been here I've been aware that whenever either of you come into my room you never turn your back on me. I know why it is, too, and don't think I blame you for it. But now – well, you see,' and she spread her hands, arched her fingers, splayed them to reach an octave, knowing that the gestures showed her nervousness but helpless to prevent it – 'what I mean is that I'd just feel better now that I'm going home if you both did that.'

She glanced up as she finished speaking, and this time she did see them exchange a look. Then Martha laughed and smiled. 'Well, I do think it's a little silly, but if you insist.' And she started to turn, then hesitated. And Mary said, 'Why, of course, we can if you want—' She started to turn, too, and stopped. Ellen saw that, for some reason, her request was too queer, that the very fact she had made it had broken their friendliness, that now, even though they knew they did not have to, they were thinking of her again the way they thought of the other patients, that the watchfulness was returning, not all at once, but by degrees, to their manner.

So she laughed again, more nervously than before, and said, 'No, don't. I don't want you to. It was silly of me – just a notion of mine. You don't have to really.'

And Martha said, 'But we can, if you *want* us to.' And Mary looked at her watch and said, 'It's getting late and I have all those other diets. Martha, you must help me!' And Ellen laughed again and watched them leave the room, but she did not eat any more oatmeal.

After she had drunk her coffee, she wanted a cigarette, and went to her purse for the pack, took one out of it and put it in her mouth before she realized that she still had no matches. None of the patients was allowed matches, even on the day they went home. She could ring for the nurse, who would bring her a match, and who would stay close by until the cigarette was smoked and safely extinguished, but this she did not want to do. Instead, she walked to the window, stood in front of it and a few paces away from it, so she could see through the lattice-work, looked down on the rolling lawn, the curving path to the gate, the elms. The sky she could see was the deep, clear blue of mid-summer, the leafage of the elms had darkened in the sun's heat, the clipped grass was spoiled with bare brown patches; although it was only late July, the season already had sown the seeds of its own destruction. The warmth of the day had begun to seep into the room; she felt flushed, and when she passed her hand over her forehead it came away damp. She went to the washstand and held a washcloth under the tap, then pressed its cold wetness to her face. She put on fresh powder and a little rouge, new lipstick, bending over the basin and putting her head close to the mirror as she made a new mouth. Her hair, she saw, still passed muster; her eyes were still the same transparent blue; there were very few wrinkles. Her lips were quiet, her chin forthright, her neck was not too long, her skin smooth. But what can I tell of the way I look? she asked herself – if there is change it goes on from day to day, I grow used to it, and although in months and years my face matures, coarsens, mocks its youth, the tiny advance age makes each day I never see, I never know. Thinking this, she picked up her toilet articles, which she had forgotten before, and carried them to one of the travelling-cases, unlocked it, put them inside and slammed it shut again. But when she had done this she was more than ever aware that it was just seven-thirty, that the nurse had said the doctor would be late, that even if Basil arrived early he would not be allowed to come up for her until she had seen the doctor and he had signed her discharge, that it would be more than an hour before she could go home.

Her books were packed, and so was her music – there

was not even a newspaper she could read. If she sat and did nothing she would begin to remember all the incidents of her illness, she would become morose. As it was, her happiness had not left her, she was only sensing its peril. Of course, she could open the suitcase, unpack a book – in fact, that was the sensible thing to do. But the packing of those cases had marked a significant moment, had stood for the end of her life in this room; she had not even liked opening one long enough to put her cosmetics into it. No, she would not read; but she knew what she would do; she would pay Ella a visit; she would say good-bye.

She went to the door and put her hand on the knob, turned it – half-expecting that it would not turn although she knew that they had not locked her in for months – heard the quiet click and swung open the heavy door. After she walked into the corridor she pushed it wide and pressed down the plunger that would hold it open, for this was a rule. Then she went down the long, green-walled, tiled-floor hall to Ella's room. Its door was open, too, and she walked in without knocking.

Ella was sitting up in her chair by the window, her face turned toward the sun, her great body limp and sagging, while an orderly fed her breakfast. Ellen stopped just across the threshold, waited for the orderly to nod his head before she walked to the window and the huge, ageing woman. Ella held a fascination for her, an attraction that could not be explained wholly in terms of the similarity of their names, as Dr Danzer had once tried to explain it, although she admitted that a part of the compulsion had originated in that. Last winter, when the other patient had been admitted to the hospital, she had heard the nurses and the orderlies talking about 'Ella', about her violent intervals, her

16

generally disturbed condition. And when she had first heard the name she had thought it her own, 'Ellen', and had been frightened. For days she had hidden her fear from Dr Danzer, although he could detect its effects in her personality and kept giving her word-associations and took a renewed interest in her dreams – she could smile at her panic now, but then she had thought that Ella's symptoms, which she overheard them talking about, were her own; she had thought that she was having violent episodes and then forgetting them. She had finally confided her fears to Dr Danzer and, to quiet them, he had taken her to see Ella, as he said, 'to show you that when we say "Ella" we do not mean "Ellen".'

As she walked across the room she remembered that first time she had seen Ella: the large form collapsed on the bed under an upheaval of covers, the twisting and turning of that mountainous body, the heaving breaths and the remarkably placid face that surmounted this disorder, the grey lumps of cheeks, the broad, fat lips, the open, staring, watery grey eyes. Her first reaction had been revulsion, and then relief, and then pity. Dr Danzer had told her something about Ella's history – how she had been a successful business-woman with many friends, convivial, a sport; how liquor had first been a pleasure for her, and then a passion, and now a mania. She had taken 'the cure' several times at less reputable institutions, but the last time she had gone on a binge it had been far worse than before – there had been some other complication; degeneration had occurred. 'She had never had a Wassermann,' the doctor had said, 'until a friend brought her here. She is under treatment now; but, of course, although we can arrest the disease we cannot hope to restore what has been destroyed.'

She had fallen into the habit of visiting Ella's room a few times each week, of sitting beside her bed or her chair by the window, of watching her placid face. Now she was rarely violent and she spent most of her day by the window – why she enjoyed this Ellen did not know, although she had noticed that the older woman's eyes sought and found the sun, followed it, and only on days when it was sunny did her expression change and something that seemed more like a smile than not inhabited her features. The great woman rarely made a sound, and on those occasions when she did it was a whimpering, and not an attempt at speech. But her face, for Ellen, held as many mysteries as the sea; its mask-like placidity, she was sure, was but the uppermost surface of a deep, many-levelled world of turmoil. To sit and watch those immobile planes and curves, those empty eyes, that gaping mouth, and then to return and search her mirror, inspect her own sentience as revealed by her own solid flesh, her changing mien, was to restore her faith in her own intelligence. So she always went to Ella's room when she doubted herself, when she was afraid.

Today Ella was eating, was being fed, and she knew that her presence was a bother to the orderly. But he had nodded his head, so she crossed to the window and stood looking down at the seated giantess, watching the thin youth in the white coat spoon up the oatmeal and lift it into the open mouth, watching the broad, fleshy hands grip the arm of the chair and then relax, grip and then relax, as a baby clenches and unclenches his fist as he sucks at his mother's breast. Yet in no other way was Ella childlike; rather her placidity seemed like the visible sign of superhuman maturity, expressing a god-like peace. In fact, her physical lineaments were not

18

unlike Buddha's; although she did not sit cross-legged, she was huge enough, mysterious enough. When she was calm it was as if she were petrified, her only movement the swivelling of her head as her vacant eyes followed the sun; but this motion was an encroachment, like the lengthening of a sundial's shadow, like the slow progression of the smaller hand of a clock from one numeral to the next. They say Ella has no perception of reality any more, she thought, but if this is so why do her eyes follow the sun? Doesn't this compulsion indicate a sensing of the passage of time, a knowledge of the continual, gradual destruction of life? Couldn't it be that she does know, that she is still intelligent, but has just lost the power of speech together with all controls over most of her muscles except those of the head and eyes? If this is right, then to hold her head steady and to seek out the sun is her way of letting us know her great determination to live. And, it could be, her violence is but a great spasm of exasperation, of despair, a catastrophic assertion of her plight. And, if this is so, her imbecility is a tragedy to her, as well as to us.

When the orderly finished giving the meal to his patient he wiped her face with brusque, masculine tenderness, picked up the tray and offered his chair to Ellen. She sat down in it, her back to the window, and stared at the woman's blank face, trying to envisage it as it had been when she had been a success in business and had had many friends. Her face had always been large – that was certain from the outset: you could tell by the shape of the skull and the structure of the bones. And she was inclined to believe that it had always possessed some of the mask-like qualities it had today. Not in the same degree, and with greater variety: there had been

19

a jolly mask, a serious mask, and, perhaps, a pouting mask. But Ellen felt quite sure that her near namesake had never shown her true emotions; she had been too much of an actress for that, too much of a saleswoman – and had she not been convivial and had many friends? So what she saw when she looked at her today was not disintegration, but an accretion, an intensification. The conflict that had been there all along, which Dr Danzer was certain had been the initial cause of her break, and not alcohol, was as much hidden today as it had been then, and this conflict, Ellen felt intuitively, was the core of her personality. How could one plumb these placid depths and find it? Where was the clue, the key, the entering wedge? Ellen felt she knew that, too – it was there for everyone to see – the one eccentricity, the one vestige of character: the woman's eyes and their habit of looking at the sun. Here is a person, she thought, who has found time out, for whom it holds no terrors, who is one with its destructive genius.

Thinking this, she looked at her watch and saw it was after eight. She stood up to go, not wanting to be out of her room when the doctor came, looking once more at Ella, her taciturnity, her mystery. In some way knowing that Ella had given her strength, had built up her hope – she would remember this calm one, who could be so violent, fondly – she walked past the door and down the hall to her room. Dr Danzer was there, waiting for her.

He stood by the window, his hand against one of the drapes, his body half-turned towards her, his eyes thoughtfully upon her. He was a small man, a slow man, a kind man. As she came into the room and walked up to him, she felt the same surprise that she had felt many times before on seeing him: she was taken aback once more by the slightness of his build, the smallness of his hands and head, the seeming immaturity of his features. His dark eyes behind shell-rimmed glasses had the intensity, the capacity for feeling pain, that one expects in adolescence; his mouth was impressionable, the way he held his lips conjectural, as if anything he might say was tentative and he was no more certain of his own mind than he was of others. But when he spoke, as he did now, this vagueness, this indecision, ceased. His words existed in their own right, were spoken deliberately and exactly, though quietly, implying the logic that had chosen them, the knowledge behind the logic, the intuition behind that knowledge. Ellen had always felt safe with this man, had liked him for himself as well as for the security he gave. And she liked him even more at this moment, all but cried aloud with joy when he said the words, *her* words, that meant so much to her. How he had known to say them she did not know, but that was not important; what was important was that he did say them, slowly and precisely, giving them to her as a symbol of her freedom.

'Well, Ellen,' he said, 'today is *the* day!'

She sat beside him and looked at him, not trusting herself to speak. She felt close to him – close to him as a friend. There were many things she had wanted to say, had planned on saying, at this time – she had wanted him to know how she had resented him at first, hated him, fought him with all her being; how she had come gradually to look forward to his visits, had learned from him to be wryly amused at the deceits a part of her practised on the rest of her and on him, had grown accustomed to testing all her motives, all her reasons for action, to questioning her least impulse, to

21

looking upon herself as she might look upon a character in a play, critically, analytically. But now the time had come and he had spoken first, had miraculously used her own words and expressed her own feeling, and she had nothing to say.

He was not at a loss, however. He put his hand in his pocket and turned his back on the window, so that now he faced her and regarded her directly. 'Did you sleep well last night?' he asked.

Now that he had asked the question, commenced again the familiar ritual, she could answer him directly. 'I slept very well,' she said, 'though it was a long time before I fell asleep. I was too excited, too anxious for the morning – but when I did, I slept like a log.'

'Any dreams?' He had his notebook out, and the little pencil on which the gold-plating was worn in places so that the base metal showed through.

'I didn't have a dream all night.'

'One always dreams. Think. I'm sure you can remember.'

And she thought. And she did remember something. It came to her as it usually came, visually at first, a scurrying, a slipping away, a something that was perceived, yet not known, not recognized, disturbing in its evasiveness. But she did not let it go, she refused to let it slide away, she held on to it by asking herself questions: Was it dark? – was it big? – was it someone? – a man or a woman? – what was it doing? – was something happening? – to her or to someone else? And as she questioned, the image did not disappear, although she did not know it for what it was yet, but at the same time it expressed itself in words, sometimes in syllables, sometimes in whole clauses, the way a melody would form in her head, sounding itself little by little, and she would try to identify it, break it up into intervals, phrases . . .

'What did you dream?' he asked.

'I dreamed – I dreamed' – she was sure of herself now, it was coming, she could say it in a moment – 'I dreamed I was playing. What it was I was playing I don't know – some large, cumbersome instrument. It kept crawling away from me. I'd arch my fingers at it, I'd claw at it and catch hold of it to keep it from getting away. I'd try to play it – but the melody wouldn't come. I could hear the melody in my head – strangely, I could see it dance in front of my eyes. I don't know how I can explain that. It wasn't notes I saw, not really, but a sort of flowing, a kind of sunny, twisting river of sound. I know what I'm saying is peculiar, but it seemed natural in my dream. I kept playing, or trying to play this tune, you see. And the instrument – it was a large instrument, but not as large as a piano – kept trying to run away. And I couldn't play the tune, no matter how hard I tried – I couldn't!'

'What was the name of the instrument?' he asked.

'A harpsichord,' she answered, not surprised that she had known it all the time, for this had happened often before. 'And, now I remember, it was most peculiar, although I liked it for the peculiarity – and that, I suppose, is the reason it was so hard to play the tune! – the harpsichord, you see, has only one . . . only one . . .'
She stopped and looked at him, and laughed.

'Blocked?' he asked.

'I am. I don't know why. It was just on the tip of my tongue.'

'Let's try a word test. You know, say what first comes into your mind. Green?'

'Lawn.'

'Gate?'

'Home.'

'Basil?'

. . .

'Basil?'

. . .

'Blocked?' he asked.

'Yes, I am. I don't know why.'

'Keyboard?'

'Piano.'

'Clavier?'

'Only one Basil.'

He looked at her, and smiled and looked away. He was smiling still – she could see that. But why had he looked away? 'Why did you say "Only one Basil"?' he asked.

'Because a clavier has only one – oh, I meant "manual". That was what was strange about the harpsichord in my dream – that was what I kept blocking on. *Man*-ual. Only one man. Basil. I was dreaming of Basil. And of music, and how hard I would have to practise. That was all there was to it, wasn't it? But why did I block?'

'Because you did not want me to know,' he said. 'Because Basil is your husband.'

She looked at him, startled, then laughed. He laughed, too. 'I think it's about time you went home, Mrs Purcell,' he said.

The doctor walked away from the window, leaving her, going towards the door. As he did this, something went wrong in her throat; she felt empty inside, forlorn. This must be how a child feels, she thought, when her father walks away from her for the first time, leaves her standing alone, and she knows that she must either walk or fall. And then she set her lips, made a face at

24

the thought – she was independent of Dr Danzer; she knew it and he knew it; there was no doubt that she no longer needed him. But she did take a step forward, was drawn towards him against her will, stopping only when she saw the way he stood, the way he watched her, the remnants of his smile still about his lips, his dark eyes testing her.

'Your husband should be downstairs by now,' he said, 'attending to the formalities. I'll go and see if I can speed things up a little.'

'There are forms to be filled, I suppose,' she said, not because she wanted to know, but because she wanted to talk, to say a little more, to hold to him and his waning interest in her for a few more minutes.

'The administration office must have its red tape,' he admitted. And then he snapped his fingers, 'Oh, say, I forgot! You are coming to see me next week, aren't you? At my New York office? I'm there Wednesday mornings and all day Fridays.'

'I can see you any time you wish.'

He took out his pencil again, and his pad. 'Wednesday, at eleven?' He looked up, smiling. 'It's just for a check-up, you know. We can have a talk. I think we should see each other for a little while more . . .'

'Eleven will be fine.'

So she would see him again. Now that she knew, she was disappointed. She was on a long rope that let her roam, but she could be pulled back at any time. Yet, as always, he was right. She would want to see him again.

He had finished scribbling in his notebook, had tucked the worn pencil away. His hand was back in his pocket, and he took a few more steps toward the door. But then he stopped again. 'May I ask you a question?' he said.

'Of course.' She wondered why he asked her permission. For the last two years he had asked and she had answered many questions – why should she resent another now?

'This morning, when you talked to the two attendants, you asked them to turn their backs on you – didn't you?'

'Yes, I did.'

'Why did you ask that?'

She was afraid. She could feel the rope tighten, could feel herself being pulled back. She moistened her lips and spoke carefully, remembering that her words must be assured, indicate poise, self-confidence.

'It was just a whim. I awoke feeling very elated – I would say happy, but you would say elated. I felt very good towards everybody – I still do. But when Mary came into the room, and then Martha, I could not help remembering other times. I remembered how they used to look at me, to watch me – how careful they always were not to turn their backs on me . . .'

'So you asked them to turn round,' he said. He looked directly at her, and his eyes were serious. 'You know they couldn't, don't you? It's a hospital rule that is never broken. It had nothing to do with you.'

'It was silly of me,' she said, 'and I admit it.'

'We are all of us a little silly at times.' His eyes broke away from her glance, looked down at his pocketed hand. 'Well,' he said, 'good luck to you. I'll go down and see what's keeping that husband of yours.' He walked sidewise through the door, backed into the hall, smiling at her, pulling his hand from his pocket and raising it, then dropping it, as if he wanted to wave but decided he had better not.

She watched him go, thinking to herself, what a nice

26

guy he is, what an awfully nice guy! But when she stood aside, as he had taught her to do, and thought of him objectively, she realized that his niceness was all probably just a part of his professional manner, a bag of tricks to effect a transference, that she did not know his real personality because he had never shown it to her. If I had met him at a party, if I had been introduced to him by a friend, what would I have thought of him? she wondered.

She turned her back on the door he had forgotten to close, deciding to let it stand open, and went back to the window. He is meeting Basil now, she thought; he is talking to him, first about the weather, then about me. How do they get along together? she asked herself. Do they like each other? She would have to ask Basil sometime what he thought of Dr Danzer – sometime in the future, when this moment lay in the remote past, when the answer Basil gave to her question would be unimportant, when she could ask it casually, idly. She tried to visualize them together, Basil and the doctor, one large and blond and forceful, the other small and dark and diffident. She shut her eyes so that she might concentrate, but she did not succeed in seeing them both at once. First, she would see Basil, and then she would see Dr Danzer. It was as if she saw them with separate senses and had to switch back and forth from one to the other, could never use both senses together. But it was not important, it was only a game she was playing to pass the time. She would see Basil soon. He would be coming down the hall, coming through the door . . .

Suddenly she was afraid. Something had entered the room as she thought of Basil coming through the door, something old and well known, something archaic and dreadful. She had met this thing before – although not for many months, she had thought she had quite got over it, that she need not fear its return. It had come each time in the same way, unexpectedly, when she was thinking of something else. It had fallen upon her, embraced her, shut out the light.

She struggled against it, wanting to cry out, but knowing she dare not. If she screamed, one of the attendants would come running, would ask her what was wrong, would tell the doctor. And a part of her knew that nothing menaced her, that the black thing she feared came out of her past, that she had once even seen it in a dream, clearly and distinctly, and had known it for what it was. Remembering this, she also remembered her own formula for vanquishing this terror: all she had to do was to think of that dream, spend all her efforts in recapturing that experience, seeing it fully and precisely so that she could identify it – and laugh at it. For it was not very awful really – only her father's body with the light behind it, swaying drunkenly over her crib, magnified and distorted by the shadows cast in the lamp's light; and her mother's voice, hoarse and shrill, crying, 'Don't you do it! – if you touch a hair of her head, I'll murder you!'

But even knowing what it was that terrified her, seeing it again in her mind's eye as she had seen it first in reality, as a child of three, she still had to fight its present form – the pervasive blackness that assailed her, the great, smothering blanket of panic that hung over her and threatened to descend upon her. She forced herself to go to the mirror, to look into it at her face, her bulging eyes, her straining, tensing mouth; at her hand that pressed against her cheek, pushed the flesh aside, stopped the flow of blood. And as she examined herself, held her eyes on the mirror and suppressed the desire to turn round, to look over her shoulder, she felt as if she were climbing up from the depths, struggling higher and higher, out of the dark and into the light. Her hand fell away from her face – although it left white fingers on the reddened flesh as a reminder – her lips relaxed and she managed to smile at herself. Her breathing became regular and her body seemed her own again; once more she was compact and whole, her natural self.

She stayed in front of the mirror, applying fresh rouge and lipstick, combing her hair. She reminded herself that Basil would be coming in shortly – this time as she thought these words the black fear did not strike, she was not even nervous – and she must look her best for him. This would be a difficult day for Basil – the first day in two years that he had spent more than a few hours with her. Two years was a long time; lovers had become strangers in less. She must do everything she could to make it easy for him, she must meet him more than half-way, she must stand aside and judge herself and him, as Dr Danzer had taught her to, try all along to be objective about their relationship. He will have changed, she told herself, Basil will have changed.

She had changed, too, although she could not tell how much or in what ways. Would he find her too different from the woman he had married? Would he like her now that she had learned to hide her conflicts, to face up to the darkness when it threatened her, to stand on her feet and fight back? Would he love her as he had once? Or would there still be the restraint that she had felt was due to the surroundings, her long absence from him, the difficulty of attempting to put back together the pieces of their former life for an hour or two once or twice a month? Perhaps they would never get the pieces back together again, no matter how much they had in the future. And, thinking of time, she looked at her watch, and saw that it was after nine o'clock.

Minute by minute the hours had fled until now the time of her life in this room was all but used up, would soon be forever past. She found herself listening for a sound in the corridor – Basil's heavy, rhythmic stride, like drumbeats in the symphonies he conducted. And, at the same time, she thought about the world she was entering again, her unguarded future, the causes and effects that would shape her life but over which she would have only partial control, the conditionings. She looked around the room again, the familiar, enclosing scene, the four protective walls, the door which she could open or close – letting in or shutting out the sounds of other lives – the checkered pattern of light and dark on the floor cast by the sun as it invaded the latticed window. I shall leave all this order behind me, she thought, and enter into chaos. I shall never know from one moment to the next, although I shall pretend that I know, as I always used to pretend before, what will happen, how I shall behave, what awaits me. Life lies before me, and, ultimately, death – I can escape neither. I shall have to choose what I do, make decisions; only in the largest, most indirect sense will they be made for me. Once I hear Basil's step, see his face, take his arm and go through that door, I shall have to keep on moving, acting, believing . . . believing in myself and in others.

Do I want to go through that door and leave this room and this reliable order forever? Wouldn't it be safest to stay here, to accept this known, unchanging world rather than to leave it and submit to the unknown flux?

30

She stood rigidly, her eyes shut, her hands flattened stiffly, pressing painfully, against her thighs. For an instant her mind was blank with indecision, she thought nothing, existed on the edge of her consciousness, balancing on the tight-rope that lies between sensation and numbness, thought and nullity, affirmation and negation. And then a scene flooded her vision, brightly and gloriously as footlights reveal a furnished stage – her room at home, her study, the rose walls, the long, low couch, the forthright elegance of the harpsichord. Quietly, precisely, the notes of Bach's aria sounded in her mind, and she saw herself seated at the instrument, breathing with the gentle movements of the melody, safe within another, kinder discipline. And she opened her eyes, once more unafraid, to see Basil standing silently in the door.

2

Basil had been a fanfare, a bright cry of trumpets, a skirling of woodwinds. He stood easily, negligently, his face relaxed as if awaiting a smile, his fine blue eyes regarding her lovingly. She had seen him all at once, as she saw herself in the mirror: the high relief of his cheekbones beneath the tense, tanned face flesh; the wide, fond slant of his mouth; the dramatic arcs of his eyebrows and the deep sculptured sockets that held his eyes: the stone of his forehead and the blond verdure of his bristling hair. She had stepped forward towards him, then ran, was in his arms, her head against his shoulder, her cheek and mouth against the rough wool of his coat. He had held her close to him, his arm long and tight about her waist, had kissed her head, saying her name to her as he might to himself, 'Ellen, Ellen.' When she looked up at him he had kissed her on the mouth – there had been no hesitancy, no caution – frankly and firmly, ardently. She found it hard to breathe, and broke away, but had stood beside him a little longer, her hand lightly on his shoulder, looking at him and smiling when he smiled. 'There are three bags,' she had said – knowing

33

she did not have to say anything of greater import – 'a big one and two small ones. Will you help me?'

Could she have put it in this drawer? What a key would be doing in her vanity drawer she did not know, but she had to be systematic about her search, she had to look every place, in every cranny – even the most unlikely places – if she hoped to find it. How barren a long-unused drawer looked, the stockings stiff in their dusty tissue paper, the powder that had been spilled smelling stale with the years. What a blatant, pinkish shade of powder! When had she used it? No, there was no key there. But, while she was at it, she might as well look in the other drawers.

The flagstones had been uneven beneath her feet, the handle of the suitcase had begun to cut into the palm of her hand (she had insisted on carrying the heavy bag; the two travelling-cases were enough for Basil). The direct heat of the sun had made her dizzy, its steady brilliance had made the grass seem greener than ever before, the sky bluer. At the lodge they had stopped while Basil picked through his pockets for the slip of paper he must show the gatekeeper; she had been able to put down the suitcase, to rest her hand, to stand in the shade of the elms until the man had telephoned to the main office and verified her credentials. Actually, she had stepped through the gate because the shade was deeper on the other side, had not been aware that by taking this action she had crossed the line, had passed into the world and out of the cloister; later, she regretted not having done it consciously, had even forgotten when she had gone through the gate until Basil reminded her, 'You went past it when you wanted to stand in the shade while I talked to the man, remember' – this was when they were on the bus going down the mountainous road to the town and the railroad station – was sorry that so soon she was blinded to the greater reality by the immediate demands of cause and effect.

The bus had been hot and stuffy, crowded with tired-looking people of all ages, solitary men and women, taciturn families, one young girl with staring eyes and an impassive face. She had felt self-conscious holding Basil's hand, and childishly exuberant in the face of this mass restraint. They had been the first ones on the bus, and had taken a seat in the rear – they had watched the others file crookedly down the hill and past the gatekeeper's lodge and out the gate.

'Are they all patients?' she had asked Basil, breaking a silence that had become uncomfortable, 'and if they aren't, why are they leaving so early?'

'Visiting hours start at six on Sundays,' he had told her. 'If they didn't, they would never be able to accommodate all the visitors. Each bus brings its load, and takes another away – they run every fifteen minutes all day. Sunday is the only day most people can come, you see.' He had looked out of the window at the crowd that seemed to grow thicker as the bus filled. 'Some of them are patients, of course,' he had gone on. He pointed his finger at the girl with immobile features. 'She is. I talked to her once on the train. She lives a few stations away in a town on the river. They let her go home every Sunday, but she must be back by nightfall.'

She had held his hand tighter, smiled at him, fighting down the fear that had risen in her throat while he talked. She could feel the tether about her waist, feel it tighten, feel it begin to draw her back irresistibly. And then she realized that the bus had begun to move, that the driver had released the brake and slipped into gear, that they were rolling downhill, away from the crowd that was being left (people were standing in the aisles, the driver could not have taken any more), away from the man who had thought himself next to get on, a tall man with a florid face, who shook a great fist at them and mouthed inaudible curses.

She had looked in her study, in the music cabinet, in the bedroom, in all the drawers of her vanity. Now she went downstairs again and into the library; she began to look through the desk; she would look in each cubbyhole, underneath the blotter, the secret compartment . . . 'What are you doing?' Basil's voice behind her, questioning, a little curt. 'I'm still looking for the key,' she said, turning to face him, surprised to see his face flushed beneath his tan. 'I can't seem to find it anywhere, and I'm sure I left it in the keyhole. Where did you see it last?' He shook his head and came to stand beside her, his hand resting on the desk, casually barring her from it. 'I'll look here,' he said. 'I have some manuscripts I don't want disturbed. Why don't you go to the kitchen and ask Suky if he's seen it? I'll bet you he has it safely put away.'

The train had been dirty and just as crowded as the bus. Some of the same people were in their coach, along with others: farmers and their wives visiting the city to see a movie or go to the beach, several railroadmen riding as far as the next stop, a junction, and a few she could not identify. She had wondered how Basil and she looked to these people, if any of them were doing what she was doing – trying to deduce who they were, where they were coming from and where they were going. Basil, she knew, stood out in any group. What distinguished him was the way he held himself. He always seemed, to her, at least, to be standing on the podium. His hands gripped an imaginary baton. His head and neck were stiffly erect, his eyes shifted position quickly, found what they sought, turned from it as swiftly to something else, keeping the entire car under surveillance as they were accustomed to survey an orchestra – first the strings, then the woodwinds, the 'cellos, the brasses, the percussions, the basses.

'Any new scores this year?' she asked him, abruptly deciding to abandon her game of trying to discover what the other travellers thought of her, because it was difficult and unprofitable.

Basil had at that moment, when she asked her question, looked out of the window at the mountainous terrain, the dark-veined rocky cliff-face that overhung the right-of-way. He had turned about at her words, but not to look at her, his eyes elevated and musing. 'There is a new symphony by D—,' he had said, naming a contemporary Russian composer whose works, although they had been highly acclaimed and had won great popularity, she had always thought vulgar, stilted and derivative. 'I have been lucky enough to obtain the exclusive rights to the first American performance. I intend to open the season with it.'

She had quite forgotten how different his taste in music was from hers. Not that they did not often like the same things – Beethoven, Mozart, Stravinsky – but that there was so much which he either liked, or espoused because the public liked it, which she thought insipid or meretricious. D— was a case in point. Like most concertgoers, she had been forced to listen to a number of his works, since his music had been widely performed from the very start of his career. Except for some early chamber music that had been timidly experimental, she had found it all dull. And she had often suspected that

37

Basil, even though she had never put him in a position where he would be forced to admit it, was of the same opinion. Yet he had championed D—'s works from the beginning, not the least of his fame as a conductor had been gained from his interpretations of them (he generally favoured a faster tempo than anyone else, and he took care to extract the last decibel of thunder from a climactic crescendo), so that now he had been honoured by being granted the right to introduce the composer's latest production to the American audience.

'Is it very long?' she asked.

'Surprisingly short,' he replied. 'There are six brief movements – two slow and four fast. One, believe it or not, is a charming minuet. A little ironic, perhaps – a few barbs of wit here and there. But, on the whole, melodic and beautiful.'

'I should like to see the score,' she said, knowing this was the thing to say, wanting, at any cost of pride, to avoid the old, useless antagonism. In a way, it was good that they inhabited separate worlds of music – there was no competition. He played Bach only in orchestral transcriptions, programmed Mozart and Haydn to pad out an evening of more bombastic works, to act as foils that in their drabness display the talents of a trickster.

'I am having the parts copied now,' he said. 'I understand it won't be published until spring. As it is, I have only the microfilm copy of the original.'

'I'll wait until you have other copies.' She was relieved that it would not be necessary to scan the symphony and comment upon it. If he had asked her opinion, she would have told him the truth – which, she feared, he would not have liked. Yet, by showing she was interested, she had pleased him, and she was reassured to find that he still looked to her for approval. He had taken her hand again, and was holding it more firmly than before.

Basil, she thought, I love you; but, dearest, I have never thought of you as a musician. Oh, you can *conduct* – you can force a hundred men to play the way you want them to – but with you it is a business, a means of winning fame and fortune, a chance to lead and make others follow, not really an art. I think you look at D—'s symphony for the first time, eagerly thumbing through its pages, humming its themes to yourself, not to find out what it is, to appraise it and learn from it, but to discover, if you can, how effective it can be, how you can twist and turn it to display your personality as a politician looks for catch-phrases in a speech. I think, Basil, that what you want – and must have – out of music, is a sense of personal power. You pit yourself against the orchestra and the audience, and the composer, as well. You stand on the podium at their mercy and drive them all into bondage by a toss of your golden head, a restless shirk of your well-placed shoulders, your angry glance, your stamping foot. And what about me? Why, I like to watch you, darling; I admire your trickery and allow you to beguile me. But, then, our relationship, Basil, is not a musical one . . .

A sandwich-hawker had come into the coach, his hoarse cry breaking into her thoughts and stimulating Basil to action. He had begun to gesture imperiously at the man – as if cueing in the brasses, quieting the strings – but when the man ignored him, he had to whistle peremptorily. This the hawker had heard, and he had offered them his basket, from which they chose cheese sandwiches on white bread and waxed cups filled with brackish-tasting coffee. For only then had they realized that it was after ten o'clock and they were inordinately hungry.

Suky was polite, bowing and mumbling neat excuses, but he was also adamant. He did not have the key, it had not been given to him, he had not seen it. He stood aside, muttering, angry at her invasion of the kitchen, while she searched the drawers of the tables, the kitchen cabinet. She left the kitchen quickly, relieved to be out of range of his subservient animosity.

She walked into the hall and went through the small drawer in the console table. It was packed with an accumulation of cards, and one lavender envelope, addressed to Basil in a small, cramped, feminine hand – whoever had written it liked to make a tiny circle in place of a dot over the letter 'i' – that gave off a faint scent of pungent perfume. She picked this up, saw that it had been opened, and even considered reading it. But she knew what it was – a mash note from some young admirer who had attended one of his concerts and had fallen in love with his noble back. Basil was always getting fan mail; he had probably found this with his letters, had read it on the spot before going out, had dropped it on the table, and Suky – who never threw anything away unless told to – had put it in the drawer. She pushed the drawer shut. The key was not there, and now she did not know where to look.

She stood in the hall, gazing through the front door at the busy street, people walking up and down in Sunday clothes, vari-coloured taxis streaming past in the still-brilliant sunshine, thinking of where she could possibly have put that key. She had looked in her study, in the library, in the bedroom, in the kitchen. No, she had not looked in the library. Basil had been fussy about his desk, and had insisted on looking there for her. He might have found it by now.

Turning her back on the door and the street, she went into the library again. Basil was at his desk, a score – D—'s symphony? – spread out before him. She hated to interrupt him at his work. but until she found that key she could do no work either. 'Basil,' she asked, 'did you find it?'

He looked up at her, his eyes questioning, his hand holding his pencil, tapping with it. 'I beg your pardon?'

'I asked you if you had found my key. You were going to look for it in the desk.'

His eyes lost some of their distraction as he understood what she asked. 'No, I didn't find it,' he said. And he bent over the score again.

She was not sure he had even looked for it.

They had stood far to the front of the Weehawken ferry, the late morning sun hot on their heads, their arms about each other, watching the spectacular skyline of midtown Manhattan loom closer and closer. There had been nights, when she had lain in bed unable to sleep, that she had doubted the existence of the city, of any reality greater than the four green walls of her room, the door opening on to the corridor, the latticed window with its view of the lawn and the elms. Now, already, as the ferry surged forward through the turgid waters of the Hudson and the bone-white buildings seemed to momentarily creep higher and higher into the dazzling blue of the sky, she could doubt the reality of that room, wonder if it had only been the worst of her dreams. She began to tremble with excitement as she sensed the nearness of the life this vista stood for; the bustle of 57th Street, the façades of Town Hall, of Carnegie Hall, the silence of broadcasting studios, the rose walls of her study at home, the clamour of voices at a cocktail party, the sound of a harpsichord.

Basil felt her trembling and held her more tightly.

'It's a wonderful town, isn't it?' he said. And, for the first time, he referred directly to the circumstances of the day: 'It must feel fine to be back after so long.'

'I don't ever want to leave it again,' she said quietly, aware of the petulance in her voice, but not ashamed of it, because that was the way she felt.

'Not even for a trip?' asked Basil.

'Not even for a trip.'

The ferry shuddered as it struck the slip, rebounded sluggishly, nosed forward into the wharf. A clanking noise startled them into picking up their bags and pushing forward with the crowd – the ferry had docked and the gangway was being let down. In a few more minutes they were on a New York street looking for a taxi.

As the cab turned into Forty-second Street she asked him the question she had wanted to ask all morning. 'Are you glad to have me back, Basil?'

He turned to her, his features not composed, his mouth slightly open, his eyes glinting. 'You know I am glad,' he said. 'I didn't think I'd have to tell you that. You ought to know that for the last year I've lived in anticipation of today.'

How nice to hear him say this! she thought – if only he had said it without my asking. But, since I asked, how can I believe him? Oh, I do not doubt he thinks so; but why did he need prompting? Why couldn't he have come out with it naturally as another man might? And then she caught herself, stood aside and inspected herself, knowing that once more she was looking for trouble, seeking umbrage. Basil had not said he was glad to have her home until she asked, because Basil habitually withdrew, was normally aloof. They would never be married in the sense that they would share a community of thoughts, nor would she

42

have wanted their marriage to be like that. Basil lived in his own world, and she lived in hers; their worlds were contiguous, sometimes they overlapped, but they would never coincide.

'Suky and I have been lonely,' he said, interrupting her internal discourse. He smiled ruefully. 'I'm afraid our house doesn't look the same. It lacks your touch.'

She leaned her head on his shoulder, shut her eyes. 'A few weeks will fix that. Although it may take longer,' she said. 'I shall have to practise at least six hours a day. You know, I haven't touched a keyboard in two years – I'm afraid I'll have forgotten how.'

His shoulder stiffened, his body grew rigid. She lifted her head and opened her eyes to look at him, to see what was wrong. His hands were clenched in his lap, his lips were compressed. 'Do you think you had better?' he asked. 'Isn't it too soon? Shouldn't you take it easy and rest up? You don't have to give a concert this year, you know. The public will remember you – there will be no question of a "comeback". Your records are all bestsellers still—'

She interrupted him. 'I am giving a concert in November, Basil. I've talked to Dr Danzer about it, and he agrees that I should concertize whenever I want. It's my way of life, just as it is yours. It's my function.'

'There are other ways to fulfil yourself – ways that are less exacting. I know how you drive yourself when you shut yourself up in the little room. I think it is still too early for you to do that again.'

They sat silent while the taxi sped down Park Avenue, coming nearer and nearer to their street and their house. Then Basil unclenched his hands and allowed his body to relax, turned to her and took her hand again.

'I won't stand in your way, Ellen,' he said. 'What

you want is what I want. I don't want you to think anything else.'

She lifted her face, and he kissed her. She shut her eyes to keep him from seeing the tears of anger that had involuntarily arisen. As soon as he was not looking – when he paid the cab-driver – perhaps, she would take out her handkerchief. For a moment she had thought that he did not want her to play again.

Ellen remembered thinking that now, as she stood outside the library door, after having asked Basil if he had found the key to her harpsichord. She did not believe he had looked for the key in his desk – did this mean that he knew the key was there but did not want her to find it? She walked slowly, deliberately, down the hall. Suppose, for some strange reason of his own, that her suspicion was right and he would prefer that she did not play again. Would hiding the key to her instrument keep her from playing? Of course not! Tomorrow morning, if she had not found the key by then, she would call in the locksmith and have a new key made. And had he not said in the taxi that if she wanted to practise, to give a concert in November, he did not wish to stand in her way? In the future she must be careful about her resentments, her suspicions. She must remember to stand aside and appraise herself at every juncture so that she might understand her fears and, in knowing them, dispel them.

Basil had intended to look for her key in his desk – of this she was now certain. But, on sitting down at it, his eyes had fallen on the manuscript, and the particular problem it presented; he had begun to work at it, and soon he had forgotten why he had gone to the desk in the first place. Later, when he was finished, she could ask him again, and he might admit that he had forgotten, go back and look. But if he did not, it really would not matter – although it was frustrating not to be able to open her instrument.

She began to climb the stairs, remembering one place she had not looked – her old purses. When she had gone through the drawers she had seen two of them; there might be others in the closets. Purses and keys went together, the key she was looking for might well be in one of those purses. Reaching the head of the stairs, and catching a glimpse of the study through the door that she had left open, she had to go into the small, functional room. Functional, but not in the modern sense – congenial might be the better word. There was nothing out of place here, nothing unnecessary or merely ornamental. The harpsichord stood in the centre of the floor, where the light from the bow-window fell full upon it. By its side stood a great-bulbed lamp to illuminate her page at night. The walls were covered with a deep rose-coloured paper above the low bookcases that held the bound volumes of her scores, the set of Grove's, St Lambert's *Principes du Clavecin*, Couperin's *L'Art de toucher le clavecin*, Dolmetsch and Einstein, Tovey and Kirkpatrick. A small rosewood table held a tabouret, a box of cigarettes and an ashtray, the long, low couch stretched itself in a corner; but otherwise the room was without furnishings. Standing on the threshold of this sanctuary from which she had been alienated for so long, she felt calmer, more at ease; the tight coil of her compulsion, that had been driving her from room to room and drawer to drawer ever since she had discovered the key's absence, slackened and ran down. But she remembered her disappointment a few hours earlier, when she had flung open the downstairs door and run up the stairs, when she had stood on this threshold for the very first time in two long years, her eyes absorbed with the unquestioned reality of a scene that had existed for so long only in her memory – and then she had stepped to the harpsichord, run her hand over its old, smooth surface, had attempted to lift the lid, only to find it locked – she could not budge it – and the key was missing!

Suky had rung the gong that announced luncheon before she could begin her search for the key; throughout the meal she had had only one thought – where might it be? Basil had been talkative and had told her all about his plans for the orchestra during the new season. He had gossiped about his fellow conductors, told choice anecdotes about famous soloists and their quirks, once more shown his enthusiasm for D—'s new symphony. She had forced herself to respond to his talk, to smile and laugh in the proper places, to exclaim and ask questions; but all the time she had kept thinking of where she might have put the key, trying to trace her mind back to the last day she had played the instrument – a hopeless task, for it had been a muddled day, a time she would rather not remember.

And after lunch she had smoked a cigarette with Basil – her mind upstairs in her rooms, going through drawers, ransacking closets. He had come and sat beside her, had showed her the microfilm score of the new symphony. It had seemed only a jumble of notes to her, a blurred, black page. But he had not known her confusion, had mistaken her vague effusiveness for ardour, had taken her in his arms and kissed her passionately. And she had given herself almost completely to his caresses, rejoicing in the thrusting strength of his embrace, postponing for a little while her search. It had been two o'clock before she had begun to look for the key, telling Basil that she must unpack, not yet wanting to admit her carelessness, her frustration. Yet now that she had admitted it, he was peculiarly unimpressed.

Sighing, she turned her back on the study and went down the hall to her bedroom. If she remembered correctly, she had kept her purses in the top drawer of the dresser. She opened the drawer, and was pleased to find them there: a moiré bag, a pigskin satchel, a small billfold and coin-purse that she used to slip into the pocket of her covert cloth coat, and a gold-mesh evening bag. Oh, here was another, a patent leather cube; it opened sideways, on the bias – she had forgotten this one. When had she bought it? She usually favoured more conservative styles than this. But, then, how could she expect to account for all her actions of two or more years ago, especially those of the last six months before she went to the hospital? She sighed again, and began to go through the purses.

She found coins, a lipstick and a compact, a rhinestone-studded comb – this in the patent-leather bag – two tickets to Carnegie Hall for 23 January 1944, several handkerchiefs and a number of hairpins. But she had not found the key, although when her fingers, groping in one of the pocket-books, had first touched a hairpin, she had thought that at last she had it. Joy had leaped in her throat, she had held her breath; but a moment later she had realized that she was mistaken, that the key was still lost. By now she saw the small object in her imagination; it shone and glittered before her eyes; she could count the irregular indentations in its upper edge that fitted the tumblers of the lock, the tiny notches: there were five of them, and one was cut more deeply, more jaggedly than the others – seeing it so clearly was especially frustrating, it was as if she had had it in her hand only yesterday, had laid it aside in some safe place, and if she only thought about it, concentrated on what she had been doing and why she had laid it down, she would remember where it was. Actually, this was impractical, since it had not been yesterday or even the day before that she had last held the key, but years; and she knew that when she found it – oh, was she ever going to find it? – it would not look the way she saw it now, that she would not have remembered it accurately, but altogether different. It was like searching for a passage in a book when your memory tells you that it existed at the bottom of a right-hand page and somewhere towards the end of the last chapter, so you think, all I have to do is to leaf through all the right-hand pages of the last chapter and I shall find what I am looking for. But you look through all these pages, and all the left-hand ones, too, and then you repeat the process for each chapter of the book – working from back to front, from right-hand pages to left-hand pages – until at last you find the passage. And you are disappointed when you find it, since it really does not say what you had thought it did, it is not nearly as moving as you had remembered it – in fact, now that you think about it, isn't it quite commonplace? – but what is most disturbing of all because it reveals what a gross betrayer your memory is, what makes the print blur before your eyes and a dry knot of futile anger clot your mouth, is the fact that this line is the first line of a chapter, the second chapter of the book, high up on one of the book's earliest pages!

There was no need for further search. It was late afternoon; dinner would be ready soon, perhaps; she should not work on the first day she was home. She would look for the key again in the morning, and if she wanted to play something in the meantime there was always Basil's piano. If she did not find the key, she would call the locksmith and he could make her another one. It was really as simple as that.

She stepped into the hall just as a loud, reverberating, crashing chord resounded through the house. The membranes in her ears, long-accustomed to the disciplined quiet of the hospital, twanged in outrage; a shudder seized her frame, shook her as a great fist might brandish a sceptre. Almost before the sound of punished strings had ceased echoing, a raucous, percussive melody rushed pell-mell forth, each note jostling its neighbour, cramped by a strong, crude rhythm. Basil was playing the piano.

Resolutely, her back rigid and her facial muscles tensed, Ellen went down the stairs and toward the source of the sound. As a means of controlling the angry cry of protest that threatened to burst out of her throat, as a means of overcoming the desire to turn about, to flee back up the stairs and into her study, to throw shut the door and fling herself on the couch, clamp her palms to her ears, she tried to decide what it was he was playing, who had written it, what tendencies the work represented and whether she had ever heard it before.

The piece was not by D—: of this much she was certain. It showed none of his characteristic mannerisms: his love of the long line, his extreme modulations, his intervallic melodies. Nor was the harmony spare – lean and pared – enough for Hindemith. The intent of the piece was satirical – just listen to that banal reprise! – and, occasionally, there was a lilt to it. It seemed to combine the worst features of both jazz and European folk material. But its composer's identity escaped her.

She walked into the library, still straining with the effort to hold herself in, and saw her husband struggling with the piano. His body pranced and danced – it looked as if it might be being jerked this way and that by a puppeteer's invisible strings – fought the keyboard with huge, hammering motions. And when he came to a gentle passage – this was a slow dirge that remembered the blues – instead of relaxing, he only returned to a state of readiness, as a wire, that has been vibrating but is now still, even in its stability cannot be said to be at rest, since its very shape and aspect belie the phrase. His hands now picked out the mournful notes as the claws of a crab grasp and roil the sand of a beach; suddenly his fingers poised for the attack – his shoulders hunched, she thought she could see his muscles heave under his coat – and as they dived into the ranks of the keys, like fleshly bombers strafing a column of ivory soldiers, the crude, bumptious rhythm rocked again, the melody of the dance returned, and he ended with a catastrophic cadence that hung about and pestered her even as he turned around, tossed his head and smiled at her, acknowledged her presence.

'What is it, Basil?' she asked. 'I know it – I'm sure I've heard it many times before – the name seems to be on the tip of my tongue, but I just cannot say it.'

He came to her and clamped his hand over hers, his touch gentle but his gesture authoritative. 'It's by Shostakovich,' he said.

'Of course – how could I forget! An early work, isn't it? A rustic dance, a polka. From "The Age of Gold"?'

He nodded his head and smiled more widely. How he adores my interest! she thought. He must have it,

50

mustn't he? What would he do if he were ignored, unable to attract anyone's attention? Or, worse than that, what would he do if he had to live alone?

'Have you been lonely, Basil?' she asked, shyly.

He had taken his pipe from his pocket and was cramming it into his pouch. Her question arrested the movement of his hands. 'Why do you ask that?'

'Oh, I don't know. It occurred to me, I suppose. I wondered.' She looked at him straightly, her eyes on his, to hide the confusion his response had forced upon her. His question had been the kind Dr Danzer asked: direct, unexpected, at first, seemingly incongruous, but later, obviously insight's entering wedge.

And he kept after her. 'But you were just talking about music,' he said, 'trying to identify that piece I played. And then, suddenly, you asked me if I have been lonely. Why?'

She laughed. 'The next I know you'll be giving me word associations and asking me what I dreamed last night. Honestly, it just occurred to me and I asked. Perhaps it was the way you played that quiet part. You made it sound like a dirge when it's supposed to be comic . . .'

His fingers returned to their task and finished packing his pipe. Slowly he put the stem into his mouth, struck a kitchen match against the rough cloth of his trouser. She felt that he did not believe her, and she hardly blamed him. Too many times in the past when she had wanted to lie, when her whole self had insisted that she protect it with a falsehood, she had not been able to bring it off. She could tell him the truth even yet – it would do her no harm. But it would hurt him, and uselessly; he was intelligent, sensitive, he would recognize the perspicuity of her observation, would be

51

forced to admit to himself – although he might shrug it off in front of her – his own weakness.

'You still haven't answered my question,' she remarked lightly. 'Perhaps there's a reason why you don't want to answer it?' She walked to the table and took a cigarette from the silver box, looking back at him, her lashes lowered, over her shoulder.

'Of course,' he said. 'Of course, I've missed you. I've missed you very much.'

She averted her eyes, walked to his desk and picked up the massive silver cigarette lighter that lay upon it, busied herself with the ritual of igniting her cigarette. Now that he had said what she had wanted him to say, she was embarrassed. She felt foolish and slightly wary. Not that she did not believe him – he had been lonely, he must have been lonely. But he had not said it until she forced him to, and there was something in this fact that made her wish that he would leave the room, go away from her for a short while.

Instead, Basil came over to her and stood beside her. He looked down at the desk and rested his hand upon it. 'Did you find your key?'

'No, I haven't. And I've looked every place I can think of!'

'You may look in my desk if you wish. I'm afraid I was rude before.'

'No, thank you. I'm sure you would have found it if it were there.'

He shook his head and looked away from her. From the way he held his shoulders, the unexpected slump of his bent head, she knew that he was about to apologize. Her embarrassment left her, giving place to a feeling of warmth, of sympathy. He has lied to me, she thought, and now he is sorry.

52

'If you didn't want to look for the key, you didn't have to tell me that you had – that it wasn't there,' she said.

He jerked around. 'How do you know I didn't look?'

She put her hand on his shoulder. 'By the way you stood. By the way you held your head.'

'I sat down at the desk to look,' he admitted. 'But then I saw what seemed to be an error in the part for the bassoon. I started to study it, and I forgot. When you came in and asked me, I didn't want to tell you that I had forgotten. I get stubborn streaks, you know.'

'I know.'

'We could look now. Together.'

'In a moment,' she said. She laid her face against the roughness of his coat, the hardness of his shoulder. Her hand clenched his lapel, his breath was warm and tickling on her neck. 'In a moment will be soon enough.'

*

But when they looked through his desk, they did not find the key. She was not surprised – in fact, she had expected it. After all, what did it matter? Tomorrow she would have a new key made. But Basil, his interest aroused, insisted that Suky must have it.

'It must be in the house,' he said. 'Suky has been most careful of that instrument of yours. He's polished it lovingly every single day.'

They went to the kitchen, arm in arm, and confronted the man-servant again. Suky bowed, and backed away; he was more polite than ever, but he did not have the key. Basil questioned him closely, and Suky answered in detail; his precise, aspirate speech seemed eager to her, solicitous. Yet when I asked him, he seemed hostile, she reminded herself – or did I just imagine that?

Before she could think this through, Basil had turned and pushed his way past the swinging doors that led to the dining-room and the hall. The dining-room, the buffet, the curious little drawer in the buffet where she had always stuck those things you kept because they did not seem to be quite the sort of things you threw away – why hadn't she thought of looking there before? Good for Basil! Now, she was sure, he would find the key!

But he did not. He found an old penknife which he said he thought he had lost months ago, some spare parts for his oboe, a tube for the radio. Somehow these unrelated objects made them feel sad, made them remember that they had once been younger – although they were not yet old – symbolized the difference between then and now. Or so *I* think, she said to herself. How can I know what Basil thinks, what makes him look sad (if he is looking sad – he may not be; it may only be that his mouth, with his head half-turned aside as it is now, is shadowed), unless I ask? And if I ask, how will I know that he is telling me the truth? Not that he would lie deliberately, out of malice or for selfish reasons, but just that he might prefer not to confess an emotion he would rather keep to himself. But, then, how does one ever know, since it is impossible to live inside any other skull but one's own, how can one ever tell?

Again she had to drop the discourse, abandon the question, leave her own inquisition in the lurch. Basil had walked abruptly out of the dining-room, down the hall, was standing by the stairs and was gazing at the console table.

'You looked in there, didn't you?' he asked her, without turning around.

'Yes,' she said, and he began to climb the stairs – 'I'm sure it isn't there' – and went up the stairs behind him.

They looked in her room, in the closets, the drawers, in a trunk and some old suitcases. They went through his room and even the guest-room, but they found nothing. When they had finished, their hands were dusty and her body ached, her eyes were tired from bending over, pulling out, looking, always looking, peering, expecting to see, to touch, to discover, something that was never there.

At last even Basil gave up. They were in the hall, outside her study. He laughed and drew her to him and said, 'Well, Ellen, I suppose you were right. You'll have to wait until tomorrow and have a new one made. Unless—' He stopped and looked past her, stared at the door of her study. 'You know,' he said, 'that's one place we haven't searched.'

She smiled at his egotism. 'But I did, silly. At the very start. I looked there several times in every nook and cranny. That's the one place I'm absolutely certain it couldn't be!'

He patted her head. 'Just the same, I'm going to see.' And he pushed past her, walked in front of her into the rose-walled room. She saw him go to the harpsichord – he did not gaze around, but went straight to it – she saw him pause in front of it, standing between her and it. He did not bend down, he did not touch the instrument. But he did emit a low, unmusical whistle. Then she was at his side.

The key, looking just as she had visualized it, was in the lock. She reached out and touched it; it was real. She turned it, felt the tumblers click, softly, easily, lifted the lid, doubling it back on itself slowly so as not to scratch

55

its polished surface. The two manuals, two banks of black and white steps to Parnassus, lay before her eyes. She reached forward, fingered a note, and heard an A twang its call to order. Her fingers stretched, she sighed, she played a major triad, a scale, a bar or two of Anna Magdalena's sarabande.

Basil spoke, as if from a distance, although he was right beside her: 'You know, darling, it must have been there all the time . . .' His blue eyes were intently upon her, his forehead was wrinkled, his wide mouth was partly open, expectant. In a moment he will laugh at me, she thought.

She hated him, and she slapped his face hard.

3

She had felt it before seeing it, felt the yielding warmth of flesh beneath her outstretched, clawing fingers, felt the sting of pain that set fire to her taut skin, felt her nails scrape his cheek. But when she opened her eyes – she was dreaming, yet in the dream she opened her eyes – she saw her hand outspread before her, saw, to her horror, that the blow she had struck had opened a great hole in his face, revealed a view, a distant, beguiling perspective, that peeped between the lattices of her fingers. Suddenly it was as if his face had ceased to exist, as if the slap of her hand had swept away a barrier that had stood between her and another scene, and she walked between her fingers, seeking what lay beyond, Basil, behind her, following her . . .

'That night I dreamed of striking Basil,' she said, her eyes on the slatted light and dark of the venetian blind, her ears fretted by the sibilant sound the doctor's pencil made as it glided over the pages of his notebook. 'It was most realistic. I actually felt the blow. My hand stung, my nails dug into his cheek, and then I looked at my hand and – how shall I describe this? – it was so very strange – it seemed as if my slap had split his face apart, although there was no blood, no flesh or tissue to be seen. What I saw instead was a vista, a long, narrowing perspective, and something – I could not be sure of what it was, it was too far away, too vague – something that I wanted to see more closely, that aroused my curiosity, existed there in the distance. But my hand was still between me and this – this vista – I saw it only between my fingers, the way a child peeps at a strange and fascinating sight. I remember worrying about this, thinking, "If I take my hand away the vista will be gone, but if I don't my hand will always stay between me and it." Then, before I had stopped worrying, I decided to walk through my hand – I remember smiling to myself and saying, "Now, you know, this is impossible; it can happen only in a dream" – but, despite my scepticism, I did walk through my own hand, and Basil did, too. He was right behind me.'

She paused and looked around the doctor's consulting-room. They sat in chairs that were placed at a comfortable distance from each other. They might have been friends, talking. There were some books in the room, not many. The lighting was soft and came from bulbs hidden in the moulding. Dr Danzer slouched in his chair, his knees crossed, his notebook balanced on his knee-cap; most of the time he did not look at her, but kept his eyes on the page, on his writing. She snapped open her purse and took a battered pack of cigarettes from it, shook it until one fell out, then probed with her finger to see how many she had left. There were one or two more, but she would have to get another pack soon. She had bought a carton Sunday night, and it was already half-gone. And this was only Wednesday—

'Can you remember more of your dream?' The doctor's question was put quietly, with total lack of emphasis; but it carried full weight just the same. She knew he was reminding her that she must continue, that she must leave nothing out – that there could be no evasion.

'I remember walking faster,' she said. 'I remember wanting to get away from Basil, but when I walked faster, he did, too. Soon we were both running. And yet it wasn't like any running I had ever done before. My feet seemed hardly to touch the earth, each of my strides covered many yards, but there was no sensation of great effort, I did not breathe heavily, I felt no wind on my face.

'We ran for a long time. Although I had gone through the hole because I had wanted to reach the vague object I had seen in the distance, when Basil followed me I forgot my original intention. All I could think of was trying to escape him. I kept on running and running, and it seemed that the longer my strides were, the closer came the sounds of his footfalls. Then, all at once, they stopped; I heard nothing. I ran a few more paces before I stopped, too. I turned around slowly, half-afraid to face Basil. But he wasn't there. He had disappeared!

'And, while I was still recovering from the shock of his disappearance, I began to be aware that the scene around me was changing. The distance was closing in on me. The sky, the ground, everything was shrinking, rapidly growing smaller everywhere I looked. I put my hand to my mouth to keep from screaming. I shut my eyes, thinking, "If I am going to be squeezed to death I would rather not see it happen." But I did not die. I waited a long time, expecting from moment to moment to feel a great weight begin to press in on me from all sides, to feel myself crushed in an inexorably contracting vice. But nothing happened and, after another long wait during which I gathered up my courage, I opened my eyes.

'I found myself back in my own room, standing in front of my chest of drawers. I had one of the drawers open and was staring into it, looking for something. Basil was still behind me. I remember thinking, "So I didn't escape him, after all. He didn't disappear. He came here before me, that's all." And then, as I thought this, Basil spoke to me. He said, "Ellen, why do you keep looking for it, expecting to find it? You know that you're looking for something that isn't there, that hasn't been there for a long time, if it was ever there at all." And I looked, and he was right – it wasn't there.'

She stopped speaking. Her lips were dry and her throat ached. She closed her eyes and let her head sag into her hands. Thinking about the dream again depressed her, made her want to get out of the doctor's room, out into the street, into the open air. As she recalled, the sun had been shining and there had been a breeze.

'That's all?'

'Yes. Then I woke up.'

'You are sure you can remember nothing else? There isn't some little detail that you didn't tell me because you thought it really didn't matter? These little details can be very important, you know.'

'No. That is all I remember.'

'Hmm.' Dr Danzer sat forward in his chair, shutting his notebook and laying it aside on the table. 'Let us see. One thing is certain. The beginning of the dream

60

– the slapping of your husband – was merely a re-enactment of something that had happened that day. Isn't that true?'

She nodded her head. The doctor was smiling inquiringly, as if he almost expected her to say to him, 'No, that isn't the way it was! How can you be so stupid?' What would he say if she did say that? But she said nothing, just kept nodding her head.

'And what do you think is the significance of the opening up of the wound, the running through the aperture, the pursuit?' he asked kindly.

'I suppose you would say that was a womb symbol. That I was expressing a desire to escape from reality.'

He stood up and walked over to her. 'A natural desire at this time. You must remember, Ellen, that you have been ill. You have lived in a small world, a world that was fitted to your needs. Now you are back in New York, and it is very different. A little frightening, perhaps. Oh, you won't admit it to yourself. When you talk to yourself you are brave. But when you dream at night, then it is different.' He turned and looked at the darkened window. 'Tell me, Ellen, what was the object that you saw in the distance? The thing you saw and wanted to reach. What did it look like?'

'It was a harpsichord,' she said, hating him for the way he managed to pull secrets from her, hating him for the time it took to say the words. But afterwards she was ashamed of herself and she smiled guiltily.

'So, after slapping your husband's face, you tried to run away from him to your harpsichord. But he ran after you and wouldn't let you escape.'

'And I never reached the harpsichord,' she said. 'Even after he disappeared I could not find it. And then things began to close in on me, and I shut my eyes. When I opened them I was in my room, looking in my drawer, searching for something. Basil was beside me, saying it was not there – whatever it was I was looking for.'

'What do you think it was?' Dr Danzer asked.

She thought about his question before answering. She had not told him yet about the search for the key on Sunday. It had been such a silly thing to do – to think she had lost that key when it had been there right before her eyes all the time. Why should she tell him? She didn't have to tell him everything, did she?

'Haven't you any idea of what you were looking for?' the doctor asked again.

'I might have been looking for the key to my harpsichord,' she said with impulsive honesty. He knows that if he only asks me enough questions I'll tell him everything, she said to herself. Why can't I keep a secret?

'What makes you think that?' he asked.

'I lost the key to my harpsichord Sunday. I looked all afternoon for it. I looked in every drawer and cubbyhole in the house ten times. Then Basil found it – right where it had been all the time – in the keyhole of the harpsichord. I was awfully embarrassed. That's why I slapped Basil's face. He was going to laugh at me!'

'Why do you think you lost that key?'

'I don't know.'

The doctor looked down at her, his finger pointed, touching the arm of her chair. He turned around and walked to the window, stood with his back to it, facing her. He did not speak.

'You think I lost it for a reason? That, perhaps, I didn't want to play my harpsichord? But that's absurd! Why shouldn't I want to play my instrument? For months I've thought of nothing else!'

'You've been practising hard since you came home?'

She felt herself shrink inside, draw up and contract. Somewhere the cruel teeth of a trap had snapped shut, biting into the gentle flesh of a small, warm, helpless creature. She tensed her jaws to keep her lips from trembling, spoke slowly and carefully, confessed. 'No, I haven't had the chance to practise yet. I've been too busy.'

'I imagine there are a great many things to do, especially since you've been away so long. But I am a little surprised to hear that you haven't played your instrument. You used to talk to me about how you were going to practise six hours each day. Aren't you going to give a concert this fall?'

'Oh, I shall. Every day I've intended to, but there have been so many things to do. I can't begin to tell you. The house! Everything's out of place – everything's upside down—'

She had meant to say more, to tell him about how yesterday had been such a lovely day and she had gone for a walk in the Park in the morning, with no idea in her head that she would be out more than an hour, and had not come back until dusk. Or how Monday she had gone shopping, had gone from store to store, had bought dress after dress; of how today, after she left his office, she had to go to Julio's to meet Nancy for lunch. Nancy had telephoned yesterday and asked her. She could not have refused her husband's own sister, particularly when she knew that Basil must have suggested that she call. It would have been rude.

'Everything is so strange,' she said instead, 'so different from what I had expected it to be,' she said, not knowing why she told him this, not having realized before she spoke that it was true.

'What do you mean?' he asked. 'In what way are things strange?'

'The house,' she said, whispering; 'it's changed. Oh, the furniture is all there, the pictures are in place. But when I look for something, it is never where I expect it to be. And I keep finding . . . finding things.'

'What is it that you find?'

'Little things. Nothing important. Some powder spilled in a drawer. Of a shade I dislike, that I do not remember having used. In the drawer to my vanity. A pocket-book of black leather, a queer, square purse, that I do not remember owning. Little things like that.'

'Have you spoken to your husband about this?'

'No.'

'Why haven't you?'

'He would think it peculiar of me, wouldn't he? He would think that I had forgotten that these things were mine. He might think I was accusing him, mightn't he?'

'Aren't you accusing him? Didn't you accuse him in your dream?'

'Accuse him? Accuse him of what?' She was indignant. Why couldn't Dr Danzer ever come out and say what he was thinking? Why did he always have to imply his meanings, make her say them to him?

'Isn't that for you to say, Ellen?' he asked.

'I don't know what you're talking about.'

The doctor placed his hand over his eyes, pressed it against his brow. He hesitated before he spoke, as if he wanted to make sure of what he would say next, think it over in his mind and phrase his thought exactly, make his precise intention clear.

'Ellen,' he said, 'at the end of your dream, when you were back in your own room and Basil was standing

64

beside you, when you had failed in your attempt to escape him and reach your harpsichord, what did he say to you? I could go to my notes, you know, and read your own words of a few minutes ago back to you. But I think it would mean more to you – in this particular context – if you would speak them again. What did your husband say to you in your dream?'

She shut her eyes and saw again her bedroom, the chest of drawers. She was looking down into a disordered drawer, a drawer in which powder – pink powder of a disgraceful shade – had been spilled. And she could feel Basil's presence beside her – if she looked up she would see his face in the mirror. And he was saying . . .

'He said, "You know that you are looking for something that isn't there, that hasn't been there for a long time, if it was ever there at all."' The words came out of her mouth haltingly, seemed unnatural to her lips. A part of her cried, you have never said anything like that – you have never dreamed anything like that – it isn't true! But another part of her, the cold, reasoning faculty, knew that what her mouth reported was unequivocally true.

The doctor nodded his head, 'And what do you think this means?'

'I was afraid I had lost something. The whole dream was about losing, wasn't it? I had lost something – something that was connected with Basil, something I may never have had. Although I kept looking for it as if I had it.'

She was silent, waiting for him to speak. But he did not speak, just as he never spoke at any of the difficult times. 'It has all to come from you,' he had often said. 'You know what it is, only a part of you keeps it well

65

hidden. But you only have to think and it will come to you.'

'In my dream I ran away from Basil – ran to my harpsichord. But Basil kept running after me and, even after he disappeared, I never found my harpsichord. Could it have been my harpsichord I was looking for?'

'In a drawer?'

'Perhaps it was the key to my harpsichord that, in reality, I looked for in the drawer. In my dream the harpsichord might have stood for the key, just as in life the key stands for the harpsichord.'

'And where does this lead us?'

Basil. Basil had kept running after her, had kept her from reaching her instrument. 'Could it be that in my dream Basil stood between me and my harpsichord, that Basil kept me from playing my instrument?'

'Has Basil ever tried to keep you from playing?' Dr Danzer asked.

'Sometimes I think he resents my taste in music. He likes other things. Great, cacophonous, modern symphonies. He likes D—'s work.'

'But has he ever kept you from your instrument?'

'When I was ill. Before I went to the hospital.'

The doctor smiled and looked away. He said nothing for a few minutes, seemed to wait for her to speak, to add to what she had said. But she refused to speak. Why did he place so much importance on this dream? She had dreamed many more bizarre happenings on other occasions, and he had brushed them aside briskly with a few curt words of explanation. Was he trying to find something wrong? Did he expect her to relapse? She was going to have to be very careful, to choose each word, to deliberate before she spoke.

'Ellen,' he said, looking at her again, smiling, 'you

66

know as well as I why your husband forbade you to play your instrument when you were ill. You know that playing excited you – made you worse. But you haven't answered my question, Ellen. I didn't ask you about before – I know about that, and you know I do. I want to know if Basil tries to keep you from the harpsichord now.'

'No,' she said, speaking slowly. 'He did say that he thought I shouldn't practise too much, that it was too soon for me to give a concert. But he hasn't kept me from it. He even helped me find the key.'

The doctor was lighting his pipe. She watched the ruddy flame come and go as he sucked on the stem, whetting the embers. Then he exhaled a thick, dark cloud that swam lazily towards her and made her want to cough. 'And what about the dream, Ellen? What were you looking for in the drawer?'

'Something I had lost.'

'But what had you lost? Say whatever comes into your mind. Quickly now!' His voice was all at once surprisingly sharp and peremptory.

And she responded. 'Basil,' she said, without thinking – just when she had promised herself to be most careful, to examine every word she was about to say, to weigh its consequences. 'Basil,' she repeated, dismayed at how easily her mind could become a traitor, how like an old circus dog it was, a shaggy old dog who jumped and did his trick whenever the ringmaster snapped his whip. How well you have me trained, Dr Danzer! she thought, scornfully.

'You were afraid you had lost Basil? His love, you mean?'

'Yes, I suppose.' Unfortunately, he was right. He was always right. That was what her dream had been about.

She had been afraid that Basil no longer loved her, that two years had been too long . . .

'Have you any reason to suspect that your husband doesn't love you?'

The doctor spoke quietly now, as if he, too, were ashamed of the trick he had forced her to perform. Now, if I were an old dog, he'd give me a lump of sugar and scratch me behind the ears, she thought, smiling wryly to herself.

'No,' she said; 'he has been very attentive, very loving. But—' And she could not continue.

'But there is something wrong, something has changed – is that it?' Dr Danzer asked. 'He is nice to you, he obviously loves you – or he says he does – but he isn't the way you remember him. Am I right?'

'Yes,' she said. 'That is the way it has been.'

The doctor stood up, surveyed the room, moved his hand back and forth in the half-light. When he was sure her eyes were upon him, he strode to the window, tugged at the controlling cords, threw open the shutters. Bright, blinding, yellow-white, noonday sun scourged the darkness from the room. The doctor turned his eyes away from the dazzling window, blinked at her. 'It is not the same, is it?' he inquired.

'No,' she said, 'it is not the same.' And she stood up to go because when he opened the windows in his hospital office it had always been a sign that the interview was ended.

But he waved his hand at her, indicating that she should sit down again. 'Isn't it a beautiful day!' he said.

She nodded her head. Actually, the sun was so bright it made her head ache. 'I hadn't realized how intense the sunlight was,' she said. 'I think it was a little cloudy when I came in. Or I was thinking about seeing you and I did not notice the weather.'

'But now you notice it,' he said. 'First, you know it has changed. Then, you begin to wonder how it has changed. "Was it cloud before? It hasn't been raining, I'm sure. Was the sun this bright or has it grown brighter? Perhaps, I didn't notice how it was when I came – I was too preoccupied." That's the way you talk to yourself. And all the time it is a beautiful day, but you are too worried about how it has changed to enjoy it.'

Now she did stand up. Now she would go. 'You mean that you think I worry too much about things – that I'm too introspective?'

He came forward and took her hand in his. It was the first time he had done this. He looked at her, hesitantly, as if he might look down at any moment. 'I think you are a little anxious, wary – that you have stage-fright. Don't you?'

'Yes,' she said, 'I suppose I am.'

He withdrew his hands, stuffed them into his pockets so that his jacket bulged comically. But the expression on his face was serious. 'Ellen,' he asked, 'what if your husband had fallen in love with someone else? Would that be so terrible?'

'Oh,' she said, 'I've given you the wrong impression. I don't think he has. It was just a silly dream.'

'There is no such thing as a silly dream, Ellen.'

'I mean I was just being neurotic. It isn't true. Basil loves me very much.' What he had said had embarrassed her, and she had begun to back towards the door. If she could only think of something casual to say, something about the weather. 'You know,' she said, 'I lied to you a moment ago. I did notice that the sun was

69

shining brightly before I came here. I don't know what made me say that I thought it was cloudy.'

'Ellen,' the doctor said, 'you are evading me again. Would it matter too much if Basil didn't love you?'

'I don't know,' she said. 'I honestly don't know.'

And, having said this, she was no longer frightened. She turned again and regarded the doctor, saw that his manner was as shy as before. 'You know, Ellen,' he was saying, 'your husband might have met someone during those two years. You may be right – he may have changed. You will have to face that fact.'

'I know.'

'But that isn't what matters, Ellen,' he said. 'Basil is not you. You are you. You cannot run away from yourself. You must live with yourself, take your life as it comes.'

'Yes, I know. But I really don't think – I don't know, of course – but I don't think that Basil—'

'I'm not saying he has, Ellen. I'm not saying he will. I'm just saying that you must not be afraid of change.'

'I understand, doctor. Thank you. Good-bye.'

'Good-bye, Ellen. Speak to Miss Nichols about your next appointment as you leave, will you, please? I think next month will be soon enough – you know you may always telephone me if you need me.'

She closed the door on his voice, without turning back, and walked up to Miss Nichols' desk. As she waited for the nurse to stop writing and look up, she realized for the first time that she was crying.

Julio's was not yet crowded – she had arrived a little before the popular time – and she found a table on the terrace. From where she sat she could see the zoo in Central Park, the masses of children in their brightly coloured clothes weaving back and forth, the shaggy ponies pulling gaudy carts, the red and blue balloons tugging at their cords high above a vendor's stand. It was so beautiful, so lively and appealing, that she found herself willing to sit still and do nothing but search for details in the shining scene, details that she was sure were there if she only had the perseverance to find them: the lost child – there was always a lost child at a zoo, wasn't there? – the barking seals, the monkey house.

Nancy was late; but, then, Nancy was usually late. She had never really learned to like her husband's sister, although at one time they had been friendly enough; but she did not dislike her either. To her Nancy was one of those people who make up the preponderant part of anyone's acquaintanceship, that she thought of as being neither pleasant nor unpleasant, attractive nor unattractive, whom she could ignore or accept as she wished. Basil was fond of Nancy, and for this reason she had used to see her frequently, and now probably would again. Nancy was brusque and unfeminine, careless and off-hand, chattering. Sometimes her aimless talk was like a knife drawn across a china plate: it set her teeth on edge. She hoped that today would not be one of those times, today, when the sight of the zoo made her feel rested and acquiescent, when she would be so glad to leave off thinking, to detach herself from the bustle of the city and the problems of her return to life.

The waiter came, and she ordered a drink, something cooling and frothy which she had often seen others have but until that moment had not had the gumption to ask for herself. And as she turned her gaze back to the park, settled her vision once more on the kaleidoscope of children and animals, balloons and buildings, a small wisp of pink caught her eye and a thready shriek, interrupted by the gusty breeze, pricked her ear. She saw the blue coat, the foreshortened, stooping back of a policeman bending down to comfort a small girl, a child with gold curls and a tam, stalk-like legs and a starchy dress. The little girl was lost – who could doubt it? – the policeman had found her; perhaps her cries had led him to her. Now he was patting her head, consoling her, telling her not to worry, that everything would be all right, that mama would come for her soon.

The waiter set her drink down on the table, and she turned her eyes away from the scene to take a sip, to taste it and see if she was going to like it, to be disappointed because it was so sweet. When she looked back, the wisp of pink and the patch of blue were gone, the kaleidoscope had whirled again and a different pattern met her eye. She felt sad and, almost, bereft. The lost child, for the briefest of instants, had been a part of her; they had shared an alienation, been united in distress. But now the spell was broken and the park became just another park with a small, cluttered zoo, and she was a silly woman, wasting time while waiting for a friend, drinking a sweet concoction that she did not like and should have known better than to order.

'Darling! You look so sad, and on such a sunny day, too. Whatever is the matter?' Nancy had arrived, her hands flying in wild gestures as she spoke, her eyes inquiring and aggressive, her teeth clenching an over-long jade holder from which a half-burnt cigarette drooped. 'Whatever are you drinking? Pop?'

Nancy flopped down on the chair on the opposite side of the small, green, metal table, crouched and began to fumble with something. She kept making cooing noises, saying, 'Now, now, sweetums – hold still! – now, ooh, isn't he the sweetest thing! – hold still, damn you – there, there!' Ellen looked over the table to see what was happening, and only then did she realize that Nancy had brought her dog along, a small animal of some obscure breed with outlandish ears and a frisky disposition. Nancy was busily tying a leash to one of the table-legs while her pet fretted at it, chewed her hand, growled playfully. 'That's Dangerous,' said Nancy. 'Isn't he sweet?'

'Why do you call him Dangerous?' she asked. 'He looks like he is only a puppy to me.'

Nancy had at last fastened the leash to the table, and now she assumed a proper posture. 'He is only a puppy,' she said. 'He is only six months old. But he is Dangerous all the same. He likes to chew my canvas and paint-brushes. He has a frightful temper.'

This was going to be worse than she had supposed. Had Nancy been this exuberant before? Or was she putting on a show for her, hiding her embarrassment at meeting her again after – after what had happened? She remembered that during all the time she had been at the hospital Nancy had not been to see her once. Not that she had minded. There had been days when she could not have coped with Nancy. But she could not keep from wondering why.

'How have you been, darling? It's so good to see you – it's been such an age! And what is that you're having? You didn't tell me, you know – although I asked. If it's really good I think I'll have one, too. It's such a pretty colour.'

She told her the name of the drink and that she did not recommend it. Nancy beckoned a waiter to her and ordered a martini, 'But dry – very dry. It must be all gin with just a dash – a dash, only a dash, mind you! – of your best vermouth. And a walnut half – just half of a walnut, you know – in place of the olive.'

Nancy seemed older, and slightly grim about the mouth. Her broad, large-featured, peasant's face, which she tried to make look feminine by copious use of rouge and lipstick, pancake make-up and mascara – but which she only succeeded in making look garish – seemed more than ever to have been crudely hacked from recalcitrant granite. Her hands, that she never quite managed to scrub free of pigment stains, now seized the menu and twisted it sideways, to catch the light, for her inspection. Her eyes swept over the printed page as they might appraise a model, noting the appetizers, the entrées, the desserts, the anatomy of luncheon. But her mind returned to her original quest, and she asked, 'Ellen, you look so sad. Is anything wrong?'

'I am a lost child,' she said. 'I am wandering through the park. I don't know where I am – how I am going to get home.' As she spoke, she smiled, taking a perverse pleasure in confusing practical, down-to-earth Nancy.

'Whatever are you talking about?' Nancy cried. She laid down the menu and regarded Ellen with frank curiosity.

She expects me to be strange, but not this strange, she thought. But she said, 'I was looking at the zoo across the way, and I saw a little girl who was lost – she was crying her heart out. A policeman found her and took her away. But, for a moment, just before you came, I thought I was that child – I felt a little lost, a little sad, myself.'

'Well! I'm glad it isn't anything more than a fancy. I was worried about you when I saw you looking so melancholy. Let me have a taste of that stuff will you?

74

I can't resist its colour. Faugh! It's positively insipid. I'm glad you're drinking it, not me!'

The dog jumped up and created a diversion. First, he had to have his head petted – then, when he began to lick her hands, she had to discipline him, to slap his muzzle and push him down.

'If he doesn't learn when he's young, he'll never obey,' Nancy said.

'And how is the painting, Nancy?' she asked, aware that she must keep the conversation going, keep Nancy well supplied with topics, prevent her from asking questions about herself. For Nancy was a painter, and not a bad one – she had had several shows – although her paintings did not sell and she was forced to live off her brother's generosity. But Ellen knew that Nancy liked to talk about her work, her great, forceful canvases that seemed to stand back and fling the fieriest hues of the spectrum at your eye.

'Oh, well enough,' the woman replied glumly. 'Although I've not sold anything yet this year. Basil says it's because I'm experimenting with Duco. The stuff they use on autos, you know. You spread it thickly on to masonite – it gives you a glistening opacity, a strength and vigour you can't get with anything else.'

'I would think it would be rather gaudy.'

Nancy stretched her hand out across the diminutive table and clasped Ellen's wrist. Her eyes sparkled. 'But, darling, it is! That's the whole point, you see. With it you can paint violently. It forces you to be vigorous, darling. You should see some of the wonderful things the Mexicans have done with Duco.'

'The Mexicans? You mean Rivera?' She tried to concentrate on what Nancy was talking about, as one listens to a parrot's garbled speech intent on discovering what catch-phrase is being cawed so raucously; but her mind kept going back to the doctor's consulting-room. Until now she had forced herself not to think of what the doctor had said, had kept herself from trying to unravel the hidden meaning in his allegory of the sunshine and the changing weather. But it was becoming more difficult, even in the face of her companion's vivacity.

'Not Rivera!' cried Nancy. 'The *real* Mexicans, Orozco. Sequieros. They have done remarkable things. Genuine people's art.'

'Isn't Rivera a real Mexican?' she asked. She remembered when Nancy had been furious about the destruction of the Rockefeller mural, when Rivera had been, for her, the greatest painter alive. Had she changed her mind? It was not really surprising if she had. Wasn't that what Dr Danzer had said? Everything changed. Even Basil. Perhaps, even herself, Ellen.

'But, darling,' Nancy was saying, 'surely you know about that? The great Diego has gone completely commercial – really, the whole hog! Of course, he was always unreliable – politically, I mean. But now he does murals for night clubs in Mexico City to titivate the tourist trade. Great, obscene, maundering things. And when one looks at his other work – what he did before – well, really, you know, one wonders. Yes, one wonders if one hadn't been taken in!'

She had forgotten how readily Nancy's opinions were likely to be influenced by current events – by politics, in fact. Both of them, Basil and Nancy, liked to think themselves liberals, although she sometimes doubted if they understood the meaning of the word. With them it was what everyone was doing that counted; they were adept at scenting out the popular attitude, the trend, and did not scruple to follow it even if it meant the

76

destruction of old gods. They were not afraid of change; but then, they had no roots. They were adrift on the sea of the present, driven on to this or that shoal of opinion by the winds of the moment, by cant and prejudice.

'I thought you liked Rivera?' she asked, to see how her friend would wriggle free from the past, how she would disclaim an old loyalty. 'Didn't you use to paint in his manner? And weren't you one of the group who formed a meeting of protest when Rockefeller refused to let his mural stand in Radio City?'

Nancy laughed and tugged at her dog's leash. 'But, darling, that was ages ago. So much has happened since.' Her eyes widened as she tried to express incredulity. 'One makes mistakes. I'm the first one to admit I do. One's taste changes. I know mine has. One grows, one progresses.'

A car backfired, punctuating her phrase and disturbing her pet, who began to scurry frantically around the table-leg – entangling his mistress and himself in the leash – barking furiously. It all made a very pretty symbol of confusion.

Not until they were having their coffee did Nancy refer to Ellen's illness. Throughout lunch she had continued to talk about her painting, telling anecdotes and gossiping about her friends, many of whom were even more eccentric than herself. Dangerous had kept barking and begging for food. Nancy had at first refused to feed him, slapping at his muzzle and shouting at him to 'Sit down, sir – down, damn you! – will you look at that! – what a pest he is!' But later the dog's constant racket had worn down her desire to train him properly and she had tossed him those morsels which she did not want to eat herself: bits of salad, a chop bone and a corn stick. After pushing them around in a greasy circle with his nose, the puppy had disdained them, too, until the waiter had stooped to retrieve them – then he had growled and snapped and created an even greater disturbance.

He was yapping again now, as they sipped the coffee. Nancy ignored him and smiled at Ellen. 'It must be good to be back in New York after so long a time,' she said. 'But tell me, don't you find everything just a little strange?'

She had been looking out at the Park, watching the trees and bushes sway in the breeze; Nancy's question startled her. For an instant she thought she was back in the doctor's office, facing the glaring sun that streamed through the window, trying to distinguish his face against the bright background. But when she turned around, she realized it was Nancy who had spoken.

'What do you mean?' she asked.

'Oh, I don't know. When I've been away and then come back, I'm always slightly dismayed to find that nothing is ever quite as it was before. The impression isn't the same; but, then, it's never different enough for me to know what has changed – if anything has changed. Doesn't it seem that way to you?'

She nodded her head. 'Nothing seems to fit,' she admitted. For it was an admission; when she thought about it she felt guilty and wanted to keep it to herself. Then, remembering that Nancy was Basil's sister, she added hastily, 'Basil hasn't changed, though. He is just the same.'

Nancy's mouth opened in surprise, and at the same time her eyelids dropped until they all but covered her eyes. She put down her coffee-cup with a small clatter and shifted uneasily in her chair. 'Is he, really?' she asked.

She pretended not to notice Nancy's surprise. She picked up her own cup deliberately and held it to her lips, but it was only with difficulty that she opened her mouth and swallowed the hot coffee. 'But that may be because I haven't stopped seeing Basil,' she said, watching her companion closely. 'He came to the hospital every visiting day, you know. He was very good about it.'

Nancy started to smile, and then stopped. 'Of course, you are the best judge of that, darling,' she said, speaking slowly and not unkindly. 'If I were you, though, I'd expect some change. Men are queer animals.'

She laughed and the sound of her laughter annoyed her because it was forced and discordant. 'You forget that Basil is so wrapped up in his music that he isn't likely to know what goes on around him for months at a time. Unless, that is, you know something I don't know . . .' She paused, trying to decide whether to ask the question she wanted to ask and, if she did decide to ask it, whether to pose it bluntly or casually as if it did not matter. Then, before she had decided, she laughed again, this time even more loudly and harshly than before. And the question asked itself – she certainly had not willed it, the words, as they came out one by one, seemed strange to her, and the voice that spoke them did not seem her own. 'He hasn't fallen in love with someone else, has he, Nancy? That isn't what you're trying to tell me, is it?' And her fingers stretched themselves compulsively, her nails scored the table-cloth, her body trembled.

Nancy's face turned serious, but only for a moment. Then she was smiling again, while she looked in her purse for a comb and a mirror with one hand and patted her hennaed bob with the other. 'Darling, how should

I know that?' she asked. 'I'm only his sister. I'd be the last to know.'

Nancy lived in a tall apartment building that overlooked Washington Square. Basil paid the rent for the roomy studio, which had great, wide windows and a sky-light, just as he paid most of her other bills. The furnishings, however, were old and well-worn; they had come from their mother's home in Connecticut and were sufficiently out of date to be fashionable. Nancy had arranged them with an artist's talent for dramatic effect – everything faced the huge windows, viewed the Square; only her easel turned its back on the sky. So, when one sat on the ponderous horsehair sofa, as Ellen was doing now, one felt as if one had been launched into space, catapulted from the earth to the clouds, delicately suspended in the empyrean.

She did not know why she had come home with Nancy. It had not been her intent to stay with her any longer than was necessary; when they had finished their coffees at Julio's and were squabbling over who should take the check, she had been on the point of remembering another appointment, of making her excuses and abandoning Nancy. There had not been another appointment, of course; what she had wanted to do was to walk in the Park, visit the zoo, wander freely for a couple of hours. Yet when her companion had suggested that they find a taxi and come down to the Village – 'I want you to see my new canvases, Ellen – I want your opinion on one of them' – she had nodded her head and agreed. It was not that she had wanted to be with Nancy – if anything she had wanted to escape her – but Nancy's mysterious manner, her off-hand warning, when coupled with the doctor's parable, had whetted her curiosity and encouraged her insecurity. If I stay with her, she had reasoned – sensing as she thought this that her reasoning was merely after-the-fact rationalization and that it was fear that was her true motivation – she will keep on chattering and may say something else that is even more meaningful, that will let me know where I stand with Basil.

But Nancy had been more taciturn during the drive down-town. After having given the address to the cabdriver, she had settled back on the seat with her pet in her lap and had passed the time stroking his back and patting his head. When they reached the tall building and had gone up in the elevator to one of the topmost floors, Nancy had unlocked the door to the apartment, ushered her into the studio, taken her hat and wrap and disappeared. Ellen was still waiting for her to return, facing the great blue deeps of sky, clotted with massive cloud-formations, that disrupted her equilibrium and all but convinced her that she hung perilously above the pit of the world, staring down into it with sickening dismay, beckoned by its immensity, taunted and harried into flinging herself down, down, down, to destruction. But I am only sitting on a comfortable sofa looking out of a high window, she cajoled herself, stretching her legs forward, making them long and tenuous, ambiguous appendages. I could not throw myself out and down from here. I would first have to stand and walk to the sill, to loosen the catch, lift and climb and heave. All I need do is to remain calm and quiet on the sofa, to shut my eyes and pretend I have not seen the sky; after all, this feeling is nothing new, I have fought it off many times before.

But when she shut her eyes, she saw the lattice-work, the diamonds of sun and stripes of darkness, the cool green facets of lawn and elms; and she remembered the helplessness of that other vista, the caged loneliness, the night panic. The blackness crept upon her, shutting out even the image of the bars, smothering her, forcing her breath to rush past her teeth, her mouth to part and moan. She opened her eyes again, quickly turning her head about, by this legerdemain avoiding the window and the immeasurable view. She found herself looking backward towards the hall that led to the other rooms, listening to a queer scribbling sound, a rapid scuffle, as if death had resorted to little feet, to rat's claws and a tinkly bell. Her mouth still open, her eyes fixed in terror, she tried to rise, to jump up, to scream. But her position was an awkward one, her body was twisted and her legs, still outstretched, acted as props rather than levers. She was caught and held, pinioned by her own limbs, a cold, anonymous hand caressed her spine, her throat was contracted and numb, incapable of speech. If I weren't so frightened, I would be amused, a part of her thought – the cynic inside her who could only scoff – for I have tricked myself into being my own jailer. But the scrabbling sound came nearer, mixed now with an aspirate murmur, a hideous snuffling, seemed behind her, every moment nearer, at her feet. I cannot bear it any longer, she told herself, her fingers prodding into the hard weave of the upholstery, her back arched and cataleptic in its effort to shrink away from the source of the sound – and she made one last effort to swerve around, remembering this time to attempt to bend her legs, striving to recall the mechanics of sitting up, of changing one's position, but frustrated again by the stiff hasps of her knees. And then the horror touched her, a cold, tiny wetness at the ankles – the black mists swam before her eyes. A coarse, grating noise, sharp like a gun's cough, broke the silence. And reason returned, mingling for a moment with confusion's retreat – as sun and rain exist together on a summer's day; she went limp and at the same moment blindly reached out a hand, felt backward and downward, still too panicky to turn – not yet remembering how to face about, reached short, bristly fur and a cold nose just at the time Nancy bustled into the room, a tray with a decanter and glasses on it in her hands, crying, 'Dangerous! Where did you go? Where did you scamper to, you nasty thing? Oh, there you are, you brute! Why, you've frightened Ellen!'

She began to giggle, her hand at her mouth to hide her grimacing lips and stifle the witless sound; her body, released from the tension of terror, went limp; she felt herself to be a grinning rag doll out of which the stuffing had leaked. Nancy turned from berating the dog, from setting the tray on a low table, to a proper, social concern over her fright, sat beside her on the high, old sofa, chafed her hands and smoothed her brow. 'He really is a nasty thing,' she said. 'What did he do? Jump at you and make an awful fuss? There's nothing to his tantrums, you know. All bluff and bluster. All you need do is scowl at him and he sulks. Just look at him now!'

And it was true. The absurd puppy, abashed by his mistress's voice, was crawling towards them on his belly, his tongue lolling, his eyes idiotic with craven humility. The sight was sobering, and she managed to stop laughing, although the obvious harmlessness of the animal that had frightened her so badly made her wonder again. Was there something, still undiscovered, that lay beneath the surface of her mind, hidden except on occasion when some accidental association – what had it been this time? the blue depths of the sky? the memory of the barred window? the blackness of the past? – allowed it to bob up into consciousness, a submerged monument resting on an unknown foundation, a landmark of her disorder? And if there were something there, something not so remote that it could, in an instant, come near and overwhelm her, how might she get to know it and, by knowing it, vanquish it? Would the old trick suffice, the pretended separation of judgement from emotion? Could she stand aside, even now, and inspect herself, lying flaccid on the sofa, listening to Nancy's cooing noises, discover the flaw and eradicate it? No, she could not; for once she was certain that it was impossible – and, what was more to the point, she did not want to.

The dog, laboriously creeping, had reached their feet, and Nancy stooped to pet him. Her touch was magic, galvanic, transforming his propitiation into ecstasy; with demonic verve he began to yelp and cavort, to chase his tail. A shower of chromatic notes sounded in her head as she watched the puppy rejoice; Chopin and his little waltz descended upon her, illogically – or was it logically? He had written it after watching just such a frolic, hadn't he? – and she was able to laugh sensibly at her fright. 'I have been silly, Nancy,' she confessed. 'Please forgive me.'

'But, of course, darling,' Nancy replied, pushing past the dog, who was barking explosively, to grasp the decanter and pour wine into one of the glasses. 'Have a little of this. It will clear your head.'

She had more than a little; she had many glasses. She sat and drank the slightly bitter wine while Nancy displayed her canvases, great red and yellow blots they all seemed – although here and there she descried something, a worker, a building, a conjectural tree –

one like another. But she nodded her head and hemmed and hawed over each; several she professed to like particularly; she even made a play of choosing one that she preferred above all the rest. Actually, she did not mind being with Nancy as much as she had supposed; perhaps it was because she had drunk enough wine to be comfortably hazy, or it might simply be that one could grow used to Nancy. And then she was glad for someone's presence; she did not wish to be alone after her fright.

A set of Westminster chimes echoed portentously, and Nancy, who was putting her canvases back in the closet, bending over, pushing, pulling, straightened up and exclaimed, 'That must be Jimmy!'

'Who is Jimmy?' Ellen asked.

But her friend had already run into the hall, leaving behind her the open closet, from which a pile of paintings protruded. Nancy's face had seemed suddenly flushed, from bending over or from embarrassment?

She turned her head towards the door, which Nancy, having opened, was now standing in, effectively hiding whoever had pressed the doorbell from view. They were holding a muttered conversation, or, at least, Nancy was. She was talking rapidly, but not loudly enough to be heard from where Ellen sat. Then, as she watched and strained her ears, the door opened more widely, Nancy backed a few steps, and a man came into the studio. She turned her head quickly – she did not want them to know she had been watching – too quickly to see anything more of him than a shock of uncombed hair. She busied herself with the decanter, pouring herself another glass of the tangy wine, and affected indifference as she heard them walk into the large room.

'Ellen,' said Nancy, 'this is Jimmy. Jimmy is one of my closest friends.'

Stubbornly, only partly out of the shyness that usually overcame her at the moment of meeting, she at first refused to raise her eyes. She saw only his shoes – shabby, brown oxfords, run down at the heels like *her* Jimmy's. Why did I think that? she asked herself. I haven't thought of him for months. Not that I can't think of him. I can review the whole past, recall every separate incident, with equanimity, even that part. Thinking this, she raised her eyes, looked upward far enough to see a pair of baggy grey flannels, the same kind of unpressed slacks that the Jimmy she had known had always worn. She shut her eyes, then opened them quickly, glanced higher yet, to see a scuffed leather jacket with a zipper down the front, a pair of tanned, short, muscular arms and large thick-fingered hands that lay placidly along the flannels, seeming to contain the thighs, as the jacket wrinkled neatly at the middle, and she was aware, pleasantly and confusedly, that *this Jimmy* had bowed. She blinked again, saying to herself: what an odd way to look at a man! – and then she gazed all the way up at him, expecting to see a new face. *But the face she saw was dead, lying on its cheek, its dark hair tangled on the pillow, its lips drawn back torturously, its eyelids half-opened, as if the dying man had found he could bear only a glimmering of sight. She gasped again and saw the black blood, the battered head . . . she turned again and tried to run but, as once before, she felt the invisible wires that held her up sag and collapse . . . it was not that she was falling, just as it could not possibly be Jimmy who was dead, who had been dead, who is dead, who must be dead, it was not, it could not . . .*

'Damn!' said Nancy. 'She's fainted.' (Her voice came

from far away and wavered, rose and fell, repeated itself.)

'Devil take it!' drawled Jimmy. 'Have ah done anything?' (His voice, *his* soft tenor, mingled with the wang of a carelessly picked guitar – contrasted sharply, in jarring counterpoint, with the steely perfection of the harpsichord's falling cadence, so distinct, so distant – his voice hummed, then sang to her against the casual chords that were not chosen, that seemed to be born):

> Jimmy crack corn, and ah don't care!
> Jimmy crack corn, and ah don't care!
> Jimmy crack corn, and ah don't care!
> My massa's gone a-waa-ay . . .

*

The strong, assaulting, pungent stench in her nostrils made her jerk her head back, made her eyes stream with tears, made her say loudly, 'Now, now, I'm all right!' But Nancy was pressing the little bottle on her, forcing her to whiff the ammoniac, saying, 'The poor thing! she's so on edge – why, just a while ago the puppy barked at her and nearly frightened her to death!' And the soft, slurred voice – *his* voice – was saying, 'Ah've had gals makeover me afore, ma'am – but ah'll swan if that ain't the fust time one's fainted dead away at the sight of me!' And she sat up straight – as much to get away from the flask of smelling-salts as for any other reason – and stared into his lean, weathered face, the face that had always reminded her of homespun and worn saddles and, paradoxically, of cramped rooms, bad air and a blue spotlight, the face she had thought no longer existed. Now, not knowing what to do, seeing that Nancy, her ministrations spurned, had gone away – probably to put the bottle back in the medicine cabinet – she winked at the face. And it winked back, slowly masking its eye, boldly, dramatically, announcing a conspiracy.

'You're feeling better, ma'am, ah trust!' he said, even before finishing the wink.

Ellen withdrew farther along the sofa and Jimmy advanced. She saw that he had brought his guitar – how like him that was! – and had laid it on the table next to the decanter. 'Yes, I'm much better now,' she said. 'It was nothing, really. I've been sick a long time you know, and I still get a little hazy, sometimes.'

'You must mean dazey, ma'am. You said "hazy".'

'I meant hazy. You see, I've been in a mental hospital.'

'Have you now, ma'am?' He did not pause, but went on with the silly act, pushed her along, maliciously. 'My grandmammy's gone to the State Hospital; but she's old and a little teched. You're not old.'

'Do we have to go on like this, Jimmy? It isn't funny.'

'Ma'am?' His eyes widened, but his mouth was tight to hold back the grin that longed to be there. 'Did ah understand you rightly, ma'am?'

Before she could answer, Nancy was back – Dangerous prancing around her, nipping her skirts – and Jimmy was on his feet again.

'Do sit down,' Nancy said. 'What a fuss you make – you Southerners are all alike! I see you're getting acquainted?' This last to Ellen.

'Yes,' she said, knowing she should say more, that it was imperative that she should say more so that Nancy, of all people, would not suspect. But she could not say anything, only, 'Yes.'

'Jimmy is quite the rage in the Village – all over town, for that matter. He sings folk-songs – the way they really should be sung, not jazzed up. You would like them, Ellen.'

'Yes.' (It was as if she had learned to speak that one word, as if she knew no other – yet it had no meaning, no phrasing, no sound; it was nothing but a mechanical action, a formation of lips, a button pressed, a light lighted.)

'Won't you sing something for us now, Jimmy?' Nancy was trying to be pleasant, but she could see that her curiosity was aroused. *She knows that something has happened, something that I hadn't foreseen – she is wondering what it is.* If he only doesn't sing . . .

He lighted a cigarette and held the match, curling with flame, uncomfortably in his hand as he looked for an ashtray. Nancy, obsequious, ran across the room – the dog barking after her – found one, ran back. Miraculously, he was saying – 'If you'll let me off today, ma'am – ma throat is sore and ah have to do two shows tonight.' He flicked the match into the ashtray, and Nancy, apologetically, snatched the cigarette from his mouth.

'Of course you can't sing! I won't let you!' she cried. 'And I won't let you ruin your throat with those things either. You're just like any other artist – never thinking of the consequences!' She paused and eyed him to see if her tirade had any effect.

He stood up, drawled, 'Ah can still plunk a *gui*tar, ma'am.' And, before Ellen realized what was happening, he had swung his yellowed instrument over his shoulder, let his large hand pass over its strings, while another depressed them at the fret. The melody began, gravely – a little self-consciously – but right, beautifully right, sounding just as it should, spacious, balanced, a form within a form, a line of thought . . .

'Why!' exclaimed Nancy, 'that's lovely! But it isn't a folk-song, is it? I mean, really?'

'No, ma'am,' he said, ducking his head – sometimes he carries the act a shade too far, she thought, but oh, does it get results! 'That ain't a folk-song. A feller told me Bach wrote that.'

She stood up. Now was as good a time to make a break as any. 'I'm sorry, Nancy, but I really have to go. My head, you know.' And she regarded him, standing, slouching, looking at her coolly. 'I'm glad to have met you, Mr – Mr?'

'Shad, ma'am. Jim Shad. Just call me Jimmy.'

She had to keep up the pretence. 'You play beautifully, Mr Shad. Do you know all the Goldberg Variations?'

'All thirty-two, ma'am.'

'Well, really, I must be going. Perhaps I can come again.'

Then Nancy: 'I don't know what I'm thinking about. Ellen, you can't go alone! Why, you've already fainted twice this afternoon. Jimmy, you go along with her – take her to her door. I insist!'

And Shad, grinning, his guitar hitched over his shoulder, said, 'I been intendin' to, ma'am.'

She did not trust herself to speak to Jim going down in the elevator or standing on the sidewalk in front of the building, the sun glinting on the varnished yellow wood of the guitar which he had leaned against one of the canopy's supports while he hailed a taxi. He said nothing, either, contenting himself with several ear-splitting whistles which brought a green-and-white cab from the rank on the other side of the Square. As soon as the taxi slowed to the kerb, she ran forward and jerked open the door, jumped in and tried to close it behind her before he could stop her.

'Drive away as fast as you can!' she cried to the driver.

But Shad was too quick for her. Although surprised by her swift tactic, he managed to grab his guitar and clutch the door just as it was about to slam shut. He opened it wide and climbed in, holding his instrument in front of him carefully, fell back into the seat as the automobile began to move.

The driver, grinding gears as he shifted, looked over his shoulder at her. 'Is everything all right, lady?' he asked.

She hesitated, glancing at Shad, saw his large hand grip the fret of the guitar compulsively, saw that his long lips were tense, his dark eyes bright with temper. Did she dare tell the driver to stop? Could she chance leaving the cab? Wasn't the sensible thing to do to talk to Shad first and find out what he wanted – how much he knew?

'Go ahead, driver. Everything's all right.'

'But, lady, you have to tell me where you're going.'

I must not let him know my address, she thought, I can't tell the driver to take me home – I must tell him to go some place else. But where? Where?

'Hotel Plaza, please.' Her voice sounded calm to her, but small and distant.

'O.K., lady.' The driver shrugged his shoulders and slumped down in his seat: he shifted gears again, and the taxi swerved around one of the curves of the Square.

'Is that where you live?' Shad asked. He did not drawl. His words were clipped, precisely spoken, lacked accent and twang. 'You've come up in the world.'

She did not answer him, did not look at him. She was afraid to look at him. But she heard him begin to whistle softly, brokenly, a few phrases at a time, the song she knew so well – that at one time she had wanted to forget but had not been able to – 'The Blue-Tail Fly'. Then he stopped whistling and cleared his throat. 'You thought I was dead,' he said. It was not a question, but a simple statement of fact.

She did not answer. Someone kept tightening and then loosening, tightening and then loosening, a velvet band around her head. All the many street noises, that were there all the time but which she had never listened to before, kept increasing in intensity – a policeman's whistle, a truck's backfire, the sound of a siren in the distance – rose to a tumultuous crescendo that threatened to deafen her. If I could only focus my eyes on some one thing, she thought, some fixed object – if I could only concentrate on that, ignore *him*, until this taxi-ride is over – everything will be really all right. But she could not look in Jim's direction; even when she glanced out of the window she saw a faint, ghostly reflection of his saturnine face, his mocking eyes, in the glass. And if she looked straight ahead, all she could see was the back of the driver's neck, his framed licence with its hoodlumish photograph, the ticking taximeter which already registered 00 DOLLARS and 40 CENTS.

'You thought you had killed me,' he said.

There was a fly on the back of the cabby's neck. It was crawling all over, now on his collar, now on the wrinkled flesh just below the hairline. Why didn't he brush it off? Surely he must feel it! She could almost feel it herself, crawling on her neck, sending cold chills creeping down her back. No, now she saw, it was not on the cabby – but on the glass partition between him and her. That was it! – the fly was on the transparent partition and at first it had seemed to be actually on the driver's neck. Just another example of how one's eyes could mislead one . . .

'Aren't you interested in finding out what really happened?' Jim Shad asked the question quietly, maliciously.

She knew that if she looked at him now she would detect the traces of a smile at the edges of his mouth, would see a deceptive friendly twinkle in his eyes. He had always enjoyed prodding people; antagonism was for him the juice of life. But this time she could not allow herself to become angry – too much depended upon her retaining control of herself. She looked for the fly again, searched for the brief area of the glass partition that she could observe without turning her head, and was just in time to see it stop flexing its legs and fly away.

'I have a big file of clippings at home,' Jim was saying. 'They're some mighty interesting stories among 'em' – he was lapsing back into the drawl and, as he did, his words seemed to grow more sinister – 'some mighty big, black, scarey headlines: headlines about *you*, ma'am, that 'ud make somebody some mighty interesting reading—'

The taxi had stopped for the light at Forty-second Street. A double-decker bus was on one side of the cab, a truck on the other – she could not tell for certain how thick the traffic was. If it were thick enough, but not too thick, she could risk throwing open the door, darting between the jammed cars, running down the street and away from Jim – losing him in the crowd. But she could not gauge the density of the traffic without looking around, without looking at him. And if she looked him in the face, she was afraid that it would be as it had been so many times in the past – that she would give in to him. She would let him do what he wanted. It would begin all over again. No, she dare not take that chance.

He was going on in that half-joking, consciously-slurred, conversational tone, his warm, musical voice having, even when he talked like this, some of that bewitching quality that made his singing simple, good and true – only what he was saying was not simple, was not good, *was* frighteningly true.

'Ah can't understand why you ain't interested in what ah'm telling you. I know you would be if you could take a peek at some of the pictures the papers ran when they was lookin' all over the country for you. I let them have some of your professional pictures – the ones you had took of you in that purty – a little scanty, but still mighty purty – blue constume you always wore . . .'

The taxi started up, bolting across the street, the driver spinning his wheel to ease it through holes in the traffic, past Forty-third, Forty-fourth, Forty-fifth Streets. Keeping her eyes fixed on the taximeter, which now read 01 DOLLARS and 05 CENTS, she decided to call his bluff.

'Are you trying to blackmail me?' she asked him.

He did not speak for a moment, a moment during which they passed two more streets and stopped for another light just short of Radio City. The Plaza is at the Park – that's Fifty-ninth Street; ten more blocks, two more traffic lights away, she thought. If I can only put him off until then – he thinks I live there, and he won't be expecting anything – I might be able to escape . . .

'You surprise me, Ellen,' he said, dropping the drawl again. She had never realized before how effective it was to have two voices, two different voices which could be used both to threaten and cajole. 'I thought you would treat your old friends better than this, Ellen. I wanted to see you again, nothing more – I wanted to talk over old times. Blackmail is a harsh word – a terrible word, Ellen. You should think carefully before you use it.'

The taxi was waiting an interminable length of time for the light to change. The velvet band was growing tighter around her skull, the taximeter ticked louder and louder, the little black-and-white wheel that turned around to show that the mechanism was operating spun crazily, seeming to go backwards and forwards at the same time. She decided, thinking slowly, cautiously, that now was not the time to speak, that she would gain time, make him repeat himself, if she kept silent.

'I can see where you might be worried about blackmail,' he said, raising his voice slightly on the last word, lingering over it as if he enjoyed saying it. 'Your husband is a very important man, the conductor of one of the oldest symphony orchestras in the world – a man with a reputation. Come to think of it, you have a reputation, too, Ellen, a good name you have to keep before your public. It's been a long time since you gave a concert – a long time since the newspapers have mentioned your name. Yes, now that I think of it, I can see where you might be worried about blackmail.' Again he seemed to pause, to weigh the word. 'It wouldn't be very nice, would it? – not nice at all – if the newspapers started printing those old stories again, I mean. I think they'd have a Roman holiday, Ellen. And there wouldn't be a thing you could do – not a thing.'

The motor of the taxi roared as the driver raced it impatiently. Then there was a harsh, rasping sound as he shifted gears ruthlessly. The cab jerked forward, subsided, the driver cursed. The automobile behind them sounded its horn, and a green-and-yellow monster of a bus nudged past them like the tortoise passing up the hare. She held her breath, the ticking of the meter clattering loudly in her ear, dug her fingers into the leather of the seat, hoping desperately that nothing had gone irrevocably wrong with the machine, that the cab would start up again. And it did, eventually, but only after another bus and several automobiles had honked their way derisively past. Unfortunately, now that they were moving again, they moved slowly, gradually rolling past Forty-sixth Street, hesitating, slipping forward, hesitating, stopping once more for a light at Forty-seventh Street.

'Yes,' Jimmy said, 'I can certainly see why you might be worried. But what I don't understand, ma'am, is why you think I would stoop to blackmail . . . ' He paused at the word, let it hang in the air.

She did not speak. The taxi was in motion again, this time silently. An opening in the traffic loomed before them, and the driver, twisting his wheel compulsively, darted into it. The blocks sped past: Forty-eighth Street, Forty-ninth Street, Fiftieth, Fifty-first – they were going even farther this time! – they might even reach the Plaza! But no, they had to beat the light to cross Fifty-second Street, traffic thickened, and they halted in the middle of the block.

'Aren't you going to answer me, Ellen?'

How could she answer him? All she could think of was getting away, escaping from the cab, from the contrasting shades of his insolent voice, from the familiar Southern drawl and the clipped, brutal precision of his other way of speaking. Seven more blocks and they would be at the hotel, seven more blocks, one – or, if luck was against her, two – more traffic lights. That was all she could think of, and she dare not talk to him about that. As it was he probably knew just what she was planning to do and had already devised a way of preventing it.

He commenced to whistle again, softly, but connectedly – he whistled 'The Blue-Tail Fly' through, and then he said, musically slurring his words so that they seemed to grow out of the old tune, 'Ah allus liked you in that costume, Ellen. It was mighty purty.'

A flush spread down her face, warming the surface of her skin even under her clothes. He was looking at her speculatively, sizing her up again, measuring the Ellen he saw now with the Ellen he had known years before, seeing her again in the brief, diaphanous costume. She wanted to look away, but for some reason she could not. Her eyes met his gaze, sparred with his, their tempers met and clashed. Then he moved closer and, before she sensed what he was about to do, caught and held her in his arms.

It was a familiar place to be. His arms were as strong as she remembered them, his mouth as frank and probing. She uncurled inside – a cat, warm and fat, walked across a room, stretching itself proudly, lazily – and met his kiss. And, at the same moment, the blackness swam in, swooping and billowing, clinging to her, claiming her, friendly, not hostile. She gave herself to it. This return to darkness was a homecoming, a yielding to placid oblivion. There was no threat here; she felt none of the dire excitement of the other times that she had fallen back into this pit, let herself go upon the surface of this sea, clothed herself in the mists of this engulfing night. Before it had seemed incalculable, formless, unknowable – a catastrophe, and she had fought against it, struggled to drive it back where it impinged, endeavoured to stand aside from it, to remain separate and by this means prevail over it; but now the sable ocean seemed bounded, had shape and substance, was meaningful – a beatitude, and she submitted herself to it, as unequivocally as she gave her consciousness to sleep, became one with it as willingly as, when a child, she had crept into her father's lap, rejoicing in her loss of identity.

Her father had been a strong man, not kind, but passionate. He had enclosed his family, locked them within the bounds of his own personality, fed them the world as he had seen it. His world had not been wide: it had centred about his store with its shelves of books and piles of stationery, its meek, maidenly clerks, its scholarly façade with leaded-glass windows and a hanging sign that creaked when the day blew gusty; but his world had been experienced intensely, for his daughter and his patient wife, as much as for himself. They both had served his clients, his wife had kept the books and paid the bills in her painfully tidy script, Ellen had dusted and polished, creamed the leather bindings, taken down the orders and done up the packages, run the errands. The bookseller had seen the great events of his day through the burning glass of his trade, the War then just a few years past had been referred to as 'the years when we stored the German stock in the cellar'. The decade of prosperity had been concentrated in his annual summer trips to Europe, which had meant long, confining hot days in the store for Ellen while she helped her mother wait on trade in her father's absence, and had resulted in crates of musty volumes, French portfolios of plates, fine bindings to be cared for during the long winter evenings. Even the happenings of the city they lived in came to them filtered through their protector's contacts with his customers: the warehouse fire, in which four workers lost their lives and which all the other inhabitants had gathered to see incarnadine the night, had been casually mentioned in conversation by Reverend Sawyer on the day he bought a set of Jonathan Edwards, and had been referred to with equal casualness by her father, that night at dinner, when he had told them how he had sold the set to the minister, how shamed he had been to find one of the deckled edges slightly dusty and how much he had got for it. All they heard of politics, of foreign doings, of local matters, one way or another seeped out of this steady flow of information on the selling of books – all they read, when they read at all, were the volumes that had been damaged that could not be sold, or those that for some reason or other incurred their master's displeasure and were cast aside as unfit merchandise. For her father had been proud of his ability to deduce when a book had been read, and the act of perusing served to lower its value in his eyes. 'Books are as perishable as butter or eggs,' he had used to say, 'and must be handled with consummate care.'

The blackness, the swirling, once frightening – but now calming – mists were intimately engaged in all this, as well as other memories: the days at school when the children had laughed at her for her affected manner of speaking and excluded her from their games because of the queer way she dressed, the upright piano her mother had inherited from an uncle, and the marvellous spectrum of sound, the ever-varying colours of notes and chords, the hushed dim silences and the clamouring, bright splendour of mounting sonorities that it had allowed her to evoke. The piano had helped her gain her freedom from the store, too, although it had not let her fly from her father, since he, for reasons as inscrutable as those that underlay his other passions – the store, his family, his upright, manly person – shared her hunger for music, standing over her while she practised, hands clenched behind his back, ready to show her a scathing grimace of disgust for a wrong note, a torturous yank at her pigtails for any indication of sloth.

He was standing over her now, as she dreamed this – hard upon her, he bore her to his will. Her fingers arched, attacked, clashed at the enigma of the keys, the old, taut strings echoed their long-spent vibrations, sustained jarring harmonies and excruciating rhythms. His shadow encloaked her; he was the sea, the night, the menacing yet benevolent image which she must fight off even as she submitted to it. And, in the background, clear and far away from the night, another music sounded, a series of graceful phrases, a pattern of notes etched in metallic tones that were above all this, complete in themselves, in touch with an ease and perfection, an essence, which was not hers then nor now, but for which she was meant, to which she was dedicated. Yet the aria she heard was in conflict with the black, engorging shadow, did not arise out of it, seemed to exist apart from it in a different time. These sweet sounds had nothing to do with the comforting pressure she felt, the warm, close darkness, the cold, blank countenance of her dead father, resting on a pillow of peach plush in a fetid atmosphere of roses, the mourning draperies that hid a relative's kneeling form. They persisted in the face of the jolting, alarming, hammering intrusion of an even stranger dissonance, a noisy, chaotic uproar that dissipated the blackness in ever-widening eddies of bright sunlight, that shaped itself ultimately in images rather than music, in a black leather world starred with a brown leather face, a wildly ticking wheel that spun black-and-white like an insane roulette table, a croaking, guttural voice that commanded her (she was aware that it was now for the second or third time), 'This is the Plaza, lady! That's where you said to go . . . you sure she's all right, buddy?'

And another voice – a soft, drawling voice she knew well enough to fear – was saying, 'Reckon she'll do. Just had a little faintin' spell, but she's comin' round. Purty soon she'll be chipper as a tom-tit. Thank you kindly for your trouble.'

She opened her eyes. Jimmy was smiling at her blandly. He had just handed the driver some money, and the man had turned his head. She started to get up, but Jimmy's arm held her own, held it down. This restraint reminded her of her predicament, added to her resolve, caused her to fight his grasp. He laid his guitar aside and helped her out of the taxi with both hands. They walked side by side, her arm locked in his, to the doorman.

'The lady had a faintin' fit,' Jim drawled to the uniformed man. 'Will you see to her while I get my instrument?'

The doorman helped her up the steps as Shad went back to the cab.

As she reached the top step, she shook off the doorman's assisting hand and turned about. Her movements seemed slow and ponderous, and Jimmy, too, seemed to be walking down to the cab with great deliberateness. The scene, glaringly illuminated by the blazing sun, was unreal, theatrical. This is not a familiar hotel, where I have danced and dined, that I am standing before, but a back-drop – the man beside me in his elegant uniform is not actually a doorman, he is only an old character actor, and that man I am watching, who is opening the door of the cab now, is reaching in for his guitar, he is not Jim Shad, but just my leading man! But as she thought this, as she tried to convince herself that the conversation in the taxi had not taken place, had been but a larger part of the dream she had had when she fainted, her cold, sceptical self withdrew and acted. She turned to the doorman – he was an old man, with a puffy red face and china-blue eyes – and said, 'That man has been annoying me! Will you please prevent him from following me?' And before he could answer her – she waited only long enough to see his tired eyes begin to kindle with indignation – she ran into the dark, cool lobby of the hotel, down a corridor she knew well and out a side entrance. Another taxi was waiting at the kerb.

She gave the driver her address, and sat back in a corner so she might not be seen from outside. Her fright was by no means spent, but she knew that she was now relatively safe from Jim. Oh, he would get around the doorman without difficulty by telling him some sort of lie and perhaps pressing a bill into his hand. But by then she would be blocks away – it was the delay she had effected that had assured her escape for the time being, at least.

For the time being! She sighed and pressed her cold hand to her brow. What would he do next? Would he go to Basil and tell him the truth? Hardly yet. He would first try to see her again – if it was money he wanted. And it probably was, although he had denied it. But then he would deny it, of course. Hadn't it always been a part of his character to do things obliquely, to force another to infer what he wanted from his actions?

But what if he did go to Basil? She reached into her bag and lighted a cigarette with trembling fingers. If he did that, if he told Basil all he knew . . . She would not let herself consider what might happen. Basil had been patient and – what was the phrase people used when they thought a man's wife took advantage of him? – long-suffering, that was it. He had been inordinately kind to her throughout her long illness. Now, just as they were ready to begin all over again, Jim Shad had to appear!

She looked out of the window and saw that she was within a block of her house. A sudden caution made her rap on the glass partition and stop the cab. She would pay him now and walk the remaining distance. By doing this she could make sure she was not being followed.

Crossing the avenue, she saw that another taxi was parked directly in front of the house. That might mean nothing, or it could be dangerous. She slowed her pace, hesitated every few feet, waited to see who was going in or coming out. At this moment the sun, which had been hidden by the western skyline, streaked red-golden fingers of fire along the street, lighting it eerily. And someone opened the door of the house and ran down the steps to the taxi.

She saw her only for an instant and in unusual light, but her profile was clear; it had the stamp of youth; the grace of her movements was unforgettable. When she looked up at the door out of which the girl had come it had closed. And when she looked back at the taxi, it was pulling away.

As she walked more rapidly to the house, Ellen could not help remembering what the doctor had said to her:

'Your husband might have met someone during those two years. You may be right – he may have changed.' When she had opened the door with her key, she went at once to the console table in the hall, jerking open its drawer and searching anxiously through the letters and cards inside it.

It was not there, although it had been there only a few days before, the lavender envelope addressed to Basil in an interestingly feminine hand. That it had been there, that she had not been mistaken, there was no doubt – the pungent perfume which had scented it still lingered provocatively in the drawer. But the letter itself was gone.

4

The lid of the mailbox felt cold and wet to her fingers as she held it down, gazing for the last time at the square envelope, her own handwriting on it, watching the rain-drops fall upon it, the wet circles of damp form and spread. Reluctantly, she released the lid, heard the noise it made as it shut. The letter was gone now – she could never get it back. Tomorrow he would be reading it! This thought pleased her, and made her glance around to see if anyone had seen what she had done.

The curving village street was deserted. The low-sweeping branches of the oaks that marched along its either side were heavy-laden with the rain, their leaves rustled with its weight, and rivulets of black water ran down their trunks. She would have to be getting back to the dormitory or she would catch her death! Pulling her slicker tighter about her, she started to trudge down the street. It was silly of her to pay so much attention to one poor little letter! She laughed at herself, and a big drop of rain ran down her nose and wet her lips, making her laugh harder. A famous man like Jim Shad would never pay any mind to a note from a schoolgirl. Still, he might – you never could tell – and if he did, if he granted her the interview for the *Conservatory News*, wouldn't that smart Molly Winters be jealous!

This hope warmed her even though the spring rain was cold, and she began to hum the aria by Bach that was her very own. She usually felt better when she hummed it, and when she felt fine she would hum it, too, because it was so appropriate. She liked the way it rose and fell, its quiet dignity, the ease with which it moved, the perfect little trills and decorations. But, and she sighed, she could never play it – let alone hum it! – the way she heard it in her head. Mr Smythe said that one day she would, that all she had to do was practise and practise and *practise*; that he had never had a pupil with such fine natural gifts. But, then, funny Mr Smythe, with his curly hair that never quite hid his bald spot, was an old dear. He just liked her, that was all.

She had first had the idea of writing to Jim Shad two weeks before, when Molly and Ann and herself had slipped out, after the house superintendent had gone to bed, and had taken a taxi to Middleboro. They had heard him on the radio before that, and had been planning to go to the Black Cat to see him for many months. The trouble was that the Black Cat, a popular roadhouse outside of Middleboro, was ten miles away from the conservatory, and the girls were not allowed out later than eleven o'clock, even on a Saturday night. It was expensive, too – it had cost them nearly five dollars the last time they had gone, what with taxi-fare both ways and Cokes at fifty cents apiece. They wouldn't have been able to go even at that if Molly had not just received her next month's allowance and if Ellen had not found out when the house superintendent went to bed and how they could sneak out through the cellar door without awaking her.

But Jim Shad was worth it. He was simply gorgeous! He was tall and thin and his face was sunburned and he had a dark curl of hair that fell down over his eye. He sang in a lilting tenor voice, real slow and easy like, just drawling out the words in a way that made you know he was singing for you. Ellen was especially fond of the songs he sang: some of them came from England and were centuries old, others came from the mountains of Kentucky and Tennessee or from far out West. She remembered one of them more than any of the others – it was the one about 'The Blue-Tail Fly'. She liked that song almost as much as she liked Bach's aria.

Today was Monday; that would mean he would get her letter Tuesday and, if he sat right down and wrote a reply, she would get it Wednesday – or Thursday at the latest. Oh, what she would give to see the look in Molly Winters' eyes right now! She would be so jealous when she saw that Jim Shad had written to Ellen! Then, when they went to the Black Cat on Saturday, Jimmy – she liked to call him Jimmy to herself, but of course she would have to call him Mr Shad to be polite – would come to their table and talk to her. And all he said, except the most special parts, she would have printed in the interview for the *Conservatory News*. Oh, it was just too good to be true!

The rain began to fall torrentially, great, curtsying, misty sheets of it danced down the dark street to meet her, the street lamps became submerged globes of cold fire. Running, her rubber-soled sneakers made queer, rhythmical squishing sounds on the flowing pavement, and the gutters, flooded by the downpour, raced and gurgled. If the rain soaked through her hat, as it had done several times before, the curl would be gone from her hair and she would have to have a new wave set in it on Saturday. She just did not have enough money for the hairdresser and the Black Cat, so she began to run faster and faster, her heart pounding, the rain smarting as it struck her face. The last block of her way back to the dormitory was uphill, and by the time she reached the low, white-columned veranda her every breath was a painful gasp. She stood for a moment on the rain-swept porch, gazing at the glistening rockers and the swing that creaked in the wind, before she scraped her feet on the coco-mat and pushed open the door.

Her father, tall and spectre-like, barred her way. Behind him she could see the narrow hallway of her home and she smelled the hot, cloying scent of flowers that pervaded the atmosphere. Why, this could not be! Hadn't she only a few minutes before mailed a letter and walked back to the dormitory in the conservatory town? Why was it that when she opened the front door of the dormitory she saw, not the wide corridor and red-carpeted stairs she was used to, not the broad, complacent face of the house-mother, but the stern, angry visage of her father? Puzzled, not understanding what was happening, she inched forward, tried to sidle past her father, her eyes on the streaks of dampness that mottled the rug as water ran from her hat and slicker.

Her shoulder was seized, clutched compulsively, and she felt herself drawn towards her father, felt the harsh, unyielding outline of his body. The hot smell of the flowers, an insinuation of decay, pierced her nostrils and filled her mouth and throat with nausea. Embarrassment and resentment made her stiff and bold – adamantly she refused to raise her eyes and look at him. Somewhere, above her, perhaps, someone was

108

playing scales, going over them again and again, each time missing the same note. Then, as she listened, she heard her father's voice, dry and rattling, catarrhal, saying, 'Shameless! You are shameless! Going out, with your poor, your sainted, mother dead in the house. Running the streets like a loose woman. Speak to me! Say something! Tell me where you've been!'

But she did not speak. Instead, the angry words with which she wanted to answer him clogged in her throat, battered against her tight lips; she pushed past his arm, ran down the hall and up the steep stairs. And he ran after her, his breath whistling between his teeth, caught her and pulled her down to him, his hand under her chin pinching the flesh, forcing her head up. But she would not open her eyes – she would not look at him – even when he began softly to curse her, to call her names she did not know the meaning of, to push her head back and back until her senses reeled and the black depths, like a furry animal, like a soft drape, like the night of sleep, drowned her . . .

She was next aware that she was kneeling in a flower-banked room, her hands pressed to her side, the thick, hot, sweetish scent of flowers all about her, walling her in, enclosing her with the thing in the casket. They had forced her to gaze at the thing, the cold, inanimate flesh that had been her mother, the pale, waxy eyelids, the powdered cheeks, the insipidly smiling lips that had never curved in just that way in life. They, her father and the minister, with soft, coaxing words had commanded her to kiss those lips, insisted that she know that chill. Then, with the murmuring of friends and relations at her back, the murmuring of a Roman crowd in an amphitheatre awaiting the spectacle, she had sunk trembling to her knees, had closed her eyes but refused to clasp her hands to simulate prayer, had held them rigid to her sides while the resonance of the minister's voice above her intoned the eulogy.

'. . . a good woman who has walked with us, a woman we have all known and cherished, a woman who has cared for her child, nurturing her, protecting her and now, having reached her allotted span, has surrendered the bowl of life to this child, bade her drink from it, bade her live the good life she has lived, do as she has done, be her mother's daughter and to live in God's presence all her days . . .'

The words horrified her, swam in her head like great, ugly, murdering monsters. Her eyes still closed, her hands weighted and inert, she rose, swaying, and turned about. The minister's voice droned on, a buzzing machine that manufactured a tone, a mechanical exhalation: the mass of friends and relatives sighed, a great, mingled breath of disapprobation. She opened her eyes and confronted them, the blobs of cloth, the bulges of legs and arms, the bobbing pink balloons that were their faces. She confronted them for an instant as the starch of terror ran through her veins, immobilizing her, making her a fitting companion to the thing in the casket. Then she fled down the aisle, past the neighbour's child dawdling on the piano stool, out into the hall, up the narrow stairs. As she reached the landing, she heard her father call, heard his anger echo and rebound in time, begin its existence in limbo. And she knew that it was already too late to return, that, having fled, she must continue to flee; that, once having left that scene, she would not go back and be a part of it again. But she ran on, down the second-floor corridor, which she did not even pause to inspect, throwing it open with a wild gesture, propelled through it by her fear. And she found herself, not in her room at home, but in her room in the dormitory – safe in the dim darkness of a familiar place that had yet to know her father's wrath, apart in distance as well as time from the house where she had passed her childhood, the place of rage and death, the sweet miasma of funeral flowers.

Molly Winters, her room-mate, was sitting at the desk, her head pillowed in her hand, asleep over the text-book on orchestration that she had been studying. On impulse, she slammed the door, causing Molly to jump into frightened wakefulness, to demand reproachfully, 'Where have you been?'

'I went out to mail a letter. It's raining very hard.'

She went to the closet and hung her streaming coat and hat, fluffed her wet hair with her hands and walked to the mirror to see if the wave was gone. No, it was still there – although she did look bedraggled! She began to brush her hair vigorously to dry it, ignoring Molly, who continued to stare at her as if she had never seen her before and never would again. The silly girl, she thought; wouldn't she be jealous if she knew I'd written Jimmy Shad!

'Ellen, I won't be able to go to the Black Cat with you Saturday.' Molly spoke hesitantly, wistfully. 'My parents are visiting me this week-end. I got their letter this afternoon.'

She went on brushing her hair as if she had not heard, although her pulse had quickened at Molly's words. If Molly could not go, that would mean that Ann wouldn't go – Ann would never go any place unless Molly went, too. And if Ann did not go, she would have to go alone or not at all. She had yet to go to a night club by herself, and she did not want to now; it was not nice. But she

111

had mailed that letter to Shad – if she did not go, she would miss her chance of meeting him. On the other hand, if she did go she could see him alone without either Ann or Molly to interfere. She was going to go, that was all there was to it! She brushed her hair more rapidly, more vigorously.

'Is Ann still going?' she asked causually, trying to keep her rising excitement out of her voice.

In the mirror she saw her room-mate make a grimace of distaste. 'Ann said she wouldn't go if I wasn't going. I tried to persuade her, but, you know, I don't think she's really interested. Ann's just a tag-along – she hasn't any gumption. I'm sorry, Ellen – I know you wanted to go.'

She saw the smile that hesitated on Molly's face before she replaced it carefully with a more contrite look. Why, she is pleased that she is spoiling my plans! I'll show her! And, without missing a stroke of the brush, she said, 'I'm going anyway. Someone will have to use the reservation.'

'But, Ellen, you can't!' Molly's tone was desperate. 'You can't go there alone. What would people say if they saw you?'

'What would people say if we had all gone and they had seen us?' She turned about and looked at her roommate, enjoying her discomfort. 'You know as well as I do that no one from the conservatory is supposed to go to the Black Cat. The dean posted a notice on the bulletin board about it. What difference does it make if I go alone?'

Molly stood up and went over to her bed and fell upon it. She began to pound the pillow with her fist. 'Ellen, you can't do it. Nice girls don't go places like that alone. You just want to get him to yourself, that's all!'

112

She had finished brushing her hair, but she continued to look into the mirror. Molly had sat up again and was looking at her back reproachfully, her mouth compressed, her eyes bright with excitement. 'What if I do want to be alone with him?' she asked her. 'What's wrong with that?'

Molly said nothing. She stood up abruptly and went over to the dresser, pushing past Ellen rudely. She picked up a lipstick and smeared her mouth with it, then patted at her cheeks with rouge. Then she turned around and grabbed her coat out of the closet, went to the door and jerked it open angrily.

'If you're going out, you'd better know it's raining,' Ellen called after her. But the door slammed on her words. She looked back into the mirror and smiled at her own reflection.

As she looked at her own face in the glass, it began to darken, to pulsate and widen. And in the distance on the edge of her hearing, an orchestra sounded, wild, discordant, yet syncopated, the regular beat of a drum, the faint cries of saxophones, the shrilling of trumpets. She leaned forward to see her own face more plainly; but the closer she came to the quickly blackening glass, the fainter and more indistinct her own image became. Then, while she watched, the mirror seemed to dissolve, to lap away as tide recedes from a moonlit beach, revealing a depth, an emptiness, a greatly enlarged interior. Before she was wholly aware of what was happening, this huge area seemed to move forward, to surround her and enclose her – and she found herself seated at a table in the midst of a darkened ballroom, her eyes fixed on a point in space not far from her where a spotlight stroked a silver circle on the floor. All about her couples sat and talked; she heard the tinkle of glasses, and the soft, amorous voices of men, the hushed whisperings and feckless laughter of women; the air was smoke-laden and close and the glass in her hand was cold and wet. Yet she did not feel uncomfortable, or even alienated – her body trembled with eagerness, and the coaxing beat of the music that had ended only a moment before was now replaced with an expectancy, an urgent desire to experience what was about to occur.

A hand clapped, and then another, and another. Soon a mounting roar of applause added to her tenseness as she struck her own palms together, contributing her own sound to the mass propitiation. The silver spotlight wavered and shimmered, then suddenly streaked across the floor to the far end of the bandstand; there it picked out a tall, bowing form and the yellow varnish of a guitar. Someone whistled, and a woman on the other side of the great room cried, 'That's my Jimmy!' The tall figure seemed almost shy and self-effacing. He stood clumsily at the edge of the spotlight, smiling hesitantly at the crowd for another moment before he walked to the centre of the dance-floor with long, loping strides, dragging his guitar behind him. A microphone, glittering in the harsh spotlight, descended on a wire until it hovered in front of him. He looked at it undecidedly and then reached up and caressed it with his hand. 'Hullo folks,' he said into it, and the loudspeaker spoke too, magnifying his soft tenor, throwing it into the corners of the smoky room. 'Hullo folks,' he said again, once more idly caressing the microphone, smiling placatingly at it as if it abashed him, 'ah've come to sing you a song or so. The kind you like, ah reckon.'

And before he had finished speaking, before the softly slurred syllables had ceased echoing, the crowd's roar

114

of welcome had died, and in its place there existed an unnatural quiet, as if some ponderous animal had quit its snuffling and scuffling, had commenced to listen, to be aware, to perceive. This quiet deepened until it was an oppressive silence, as if the tall man at the microphone had thrown a spell on the room. He stood there, smiling to himself, wilfully enjoying his mastery of the crowd, the animal. His eyes glinted in the spotlight, which picked him mercilessly out of the surrounding dark – he knew that soon he must sing, that the wild creature out there demanded it, but that it was also his function to hold it at bay as long as possible. The silence seemed to have been stretched to the breaking point; it seemed that if another instant should pass the tension would be too great, a horrifying roar would burst loose from the animal's thousand throats – it was at this point that Jim Shad chose to sing.

He sang quietly, as softly as he had spoken, and it was as if he sang to her. What he sang did not matter; she did not listen to the words, nor did she follow the melody, sort out its rhythm, its structure, its cadence. Yet his song had more meaning for her than any music had ever had before; it had the effect of an incantation, a direct magic that transformed her. As he sang, she fingered his letter, which had arrived only that morning, his invitation to meet him at the bar after his performance, to go to some quiet place where they could talk. Her throat went dry as he ended one song and began another, a quicker, jauntier one, and her cheeks burned as she remembered that she had not told Molly or Ann about the letter, that she had known they would not have approved of her meeting a man without an escort, that they would have insisted that she did not go out with him alone. But why should she worry about what they thought? – she was old enough to know what she was doing, wasn't she? All she knew was that he had written to her, that he wanted to meet her and talk to her, that he was singing for her now.

As he finished his second song, and the dark, restive audience began to pound the tables and applaud, as the silver spotlight turned and his fingers experimentally plucked a few strange chords on his guitar, she rose and pushed her way through the crooked aisle of chairs back to the bar. She could still see him from there, could still hear his plaintive voice as it related the story of 'The Blue-Tail Fly', but his figure had shrunk, had become impersonal, her heart's frenzied pulsations had subsided, and she found she could breathe more easily. To stand at the bar she had to buy a drink, and it was her third one of the evening – she sipped it slowly, but despite this caution she soon felt pleasantly silly, smiling to herself and giggling whenever she thought of Jimmy and the way he had addressed his songs to her. Until finally she realized that the audience was applauding again, that she no longer heard his voice or his guitar, that now even the applause was dying away. And she knew that the performance was over and shortly he would be with her. She stiffened and held herself as straight as she could, although it occurred to her that there was something very funny, something that if she could just think for a moment so that she might know what it was she would want to laugh at; but she dare not take the time to think now, when Jim was about to appear. So she looked in the mirror behind the bartender, looked at her own face brightly reflected in the vari-coloured light, smiling ever so slightly, holding her head at just the right angle – the angle she had worked out patiently so many times before, the angle she was sure was her best angle, the inclination of her head that made her eyes seem mysterious, that emphasized the beguiling shadow that sometimes hovered over her lips, that made her seem self-possessed and dignified. And while she inspected herself, she saw him approaching, saw his tall form loom out of the surrounding darkness, saw his tanned, tight-lipped face coming closer and closer.

Frightened and shy now that the meeting she had been looking forward to all the week was at hand, she looked away from the mirror, looked down at her drink and the lop-sided cherry that still floated in it, waiting for him to speak. Behind her the orchestra began to blare and, with a scraping of chairs and a muttering of voices, the great animal got to its feet and began to shuffle around the dance floor. She was aware that he stood beside her; she could feel the warmth of his body; if she had wanted she could have brushed against him. But she still did not look up. A tapping sound, hard and metallic, made her jump with surprise – she looked aside and saw his hand, holding a coin, striking it against the bar to get the bartender's attention. Then she heard his voice, heard the sound of it before she heard his words, for an instant thought he was addressing her – as she expected him to – and, consequently, looked up at him and smiled before she realized that what he had said had only been directed at the neglectful bartender, 'H'yah, Jack! How's about the usual?'

But he had seen her smile, and it had pleased him; now that she had looked at him, she found she could not look away. He turned his head slightly in deference to her, so that his bright, brown eyes glanced directly into her own, inquiring of her why she had smiled even as his lips pursed and he breathed a long, quiet, admiring whistle. Her cheeks flushed and she felt her own smile freeze, become irretrievable, in embarrassment; for it was obvious to her now that he did not recognize her, that he could not have recognized her, since he had never seen her, that she was only a stranger who had smiled provocatively to him. And yet she could not speak, could not say the words that would clear up the misapprehension that must be forming in his mind, could not even find the strength to lower her head and look away. He took her discomfiture for boldness and his smile broadened into an anticipatory grin. 'Why, hullo, beautiful,' he softly said. 'Wheah have you been all my life?'

The only response she could make was to seize her drink more tightly, to raise the glass tremblingly to her lips and swallow it quickly, cherry and all. He raised his eyebrow slightly and whistled again, this time at the bartender. 'H'yah, Jack. What you keepin' us waiting for? This lady an' myself are prit near dyin' of thirst!'

The bartender bobbed into view and took her glass from her reluctant hand. Without it, she did not know where to look except to look at him. And what was wrong with that? She liked to look at him, didn't she? She had arranged to meet him, hadn't she? She sighed and her smile relaxed, became a little less frightened. In just a moment, she knew she would be able to speak to him, to tell him who she was and why she had smiled. But before the words had formed properly in her mind he had covered her hand gently with his own, a friendly, confidential pressure, and had drawled, 'What's the matter, honey? Has the old cat got yoh tongue?'

His question, although she knew he meant it jocularly, that he had said it only to be pleasant, had not necessarily expected an answer, unsettled her and made it still more difficult for her to speak. Instead, she poked restlessly at her hair, turning away from him as coldly as she dared to stare at the pale reflection of her own blue eyes in the mirror. But, even so, she did not escape his inquiring glance. He, too, turned and looked into the mirror, his elbow leaned against the polished bar, the image of his sunburned face above her own and just beside it, the tiers of amber bottles on either side acting as a frame making it seem that she was staring at a picture of them both, a dull and clouded picture in an amber frame, a picture taken on a dark and rainy day. Then, almost as if he had wished to make the effect complete, he put his arm around her, gently, persuasively. And he was saying, 'Why don't we have our drink an' go for a drive, beautiful? My car's parked just outside an' I hear tell there's a moon—'

While she watched, while she was still too amazed to do anything about his arm that rested so familiarly – as if it had always belonged there – about her shoulders, the mirror shivered and cracked into a million slivers, the night invaded it, the swirling blackness, and she felt herself caught up and held, lifted gently but with a firmness that was reassuring . . . she felt herself carried. Many voices existed on all sides of her, some shrill and demanding, some quieter and more resourceful, but one voice dominated them all, softly but persistently, and then the voices died away and it was quieter and cooler and she closed her eyes and gave herself to whatever it was that was happening.

Slowly the strange sensation grew stronger, gradually it took possession of her, became a part of her that was essential to her being; it was a sensation of freedom, of disassociation – she floated high above all earthly connexions and gloried in her ascension. This cannot

119

be real, she told herself, it must be an illusion. Yet for her, at that moment, it was the only possible reality. She kept her eyes closed, fearing to open them, while she felt herself become lighter and lighter until it seemed she had no weight, no substance, had changed into an essence, an abstraction. Most wonderful of all, she realized, was the happiness she had attained, the sense of contentment, of perfect, immutable equilibrium. She was at peace, at rest, wholly free of the suzerainty of time and space. And then, without thinking about it, she knew what had happened to her, and she also knew that it was what she had always desired, although she had never before had the wit to put it into words: she had become music.

Yes, she had become majestic sound, a rolling, evanescent structure that billowed and cavorted, that made light of time and space because it had grown out of them, was compounded of them, was their inevitable result. She was tone and melody and rhythmic beat, she was harmony and colour. In her the woodwinds blew and the brasses stormed, she inhabited the sweet turbulence of the strings, the intelligence of the keyboard. This was what she had longed for, even if she had not known it; this was her grace, her beatitude . . .

She opened her eyes and saw that she floated high in the air, that the moon was her neighbour and that small clouds raced playfully by her side; below, like an overturned saucer, the earth existed. And she discovered that though the world was far beneath her, she could see anything that happened on its surface, if she cared to look for it. So it was that she found the automobile, the long, low-slung roadster with its bright red body and its chromium exhausts, flying along a country road in the shadow of the clouds, *her* clouds that scudded companionably beside her. And so it was, by looking a little longer at this reckless car, by following it with her eyes and mind, by haunting it with her melody, that she discovered its occupants, the two of them: the lean, saddle-faced man who drove like a demon, eyes hard upon the black streak of road, arm thrown about the small form of the girl, the dreamy-eyed child who nestled against his shoulder, the conservatory student who had fallen in love with a cabaret performer. As she realized that this was another of her selves that she was watching, another, more tangible Ellen, a shudder interrupted the flow of her sound, a discord like a crash of thunder or the scream of a rising gale, a dissonance that was like a premonition of disaster.

Now she began to hear her own sound, to listen to a procession of mournful notes against the funereal crepitation of muffled drums, the solemn shuffle of a dead march. And, as she listened, she looked away from the speeding roadster, away from the huddled, loving figure of the wayward girl, only to glimpse another scene, to take ineluctably the next step on the path to catastrophe. She saw, below her, an ill-lit room. It was as if the roof had been lifted off and she peered down into the interior, as if she were watching a play from the heights of the stage. The time was later – this she half-sensed, half-remembered; weeks had passed, and with them many surreptitious appointments, many careless journeys over country roads. The man and the girl were in this room, the girl sitting in a pool of shaded light thrown by a lamp, resting languorously, her long, bare legs and half-naked torso bathed in its dim effulgence. The man was seated on the brass bedstead, his head tousled and his eyes red and sleepless, a wisp of smoke curling from the cigarette that burned near his lip, a yellowed instrument lying in abandonment across his lap. He, too, was only partially clothed, his brown arms and heavy shoulders bulged muscularly out of his sodden, greying undershirt, glistening with sweat. They stared at each other, the girl and the man, exposing the animosity that belongs only to adversaries who are also intimates, and the girl's bosom heaved under the dully shimmering blue sequins of her *bandeau*. As she watched from above, her eyes falling down on the foreshortened figures, the gloomy music that was a part of her swelled to a crescendo, a mighty protestation of despair – only to fall away, to cease dramatically, as the man stroked his hand over the guitar's strings and a broken chord rang out with the resonance of steel on stone. At this clarion sound the girl rose ghostlily, seemed to hover on her toes above the room's scarred floor. She saw that she was clothed in glimmering blue metalled cloth, cerulean stars on her breasts and thighs. Taut and trembling, caught at a point in the middle of her back, two fragile wings of finest wire and gauze hung in a frenzy of awkward levitation as she pirouetted. Again the man on the bed struck a broken, peremptory chord, but this time he followed it with another and another, each subtly different, each less startling, more anticipatory, until his right hand came in, too, and a melody was formed. The girl began to dance, still on her toes, still taking mincing steps, making fluttering, indecisive motions; and, softly, the man began to sing:

> When I was young I used to wait
> On Massa and give him his plate,
> And pass the bottle when he got dry
> And brush away the blue-tail fly.

Against the humming, somnolent sound of his voice, the twanging chords of the guitar, faint but clear despite the distance in time and space (for the room where this was happening was not only beneath her but in some way in back of her, too, and she felt she must crane her neck to keep it in sight, to keep from losing it, to keep from putting it some place where she might never find it again) – against this sound that rose from the room, replacing the deathly music that had been a part of her, she heard an orchestra, a brassy blare of a band, 'swinging' the melody that Jim was singing – for the man was Jim, she had no doubt of that, and the girl was herself – making a blatant mockery of it. This noise – she could not have called it music – grew louder and louder, drowning out the plaintive insinuations of the guitar, drowning out Jim's melancholy tenor, climbing up into a blasting fanfare with a flourish on the drums and a snort from the trombones. And, as the fanfare rocketed to its climax, she lost her footing among the clouds, the moon was eclipsed and the clouds turned into black spirits that hastened to smother her. Down, down, down, she plunged, oppressed as she felt weight and substance return, drawn to the lodestone earth with dizzying velocity. Falling faster and faster, the blackness commenced to spin about her, to take shape and thickness, to become solid and palpable. Terror struck at her heart when she saw a bright blue dagger of light streak down from above, fly past her like lightning, and end in a lake, an ellipse, a shiny stain of blue fire. Panic mounted in her throat, claiming the scream that had begun there, devouring it, as the shiny stain of blue crept towards her across the blackness, getting closer and closer, seeking her and knowing where she could be found, advancing to engorge her.

She went rigid, cold as lunar ice, her ankles tense, her toes arching; she balanced on a point, holding her breath, her arms out, her head back, her eyes on the blue maw. Then, as it grew near, it sprang, drenching her with witch colour and bawd light, stigmatizing her: it, the accusing hammer; she, the accepting, submissive anvil. She stood, on her point, poised for another instant, a blue houri, as she looked up and back, following the bludgeon stroke of blue to its source, a splinter of sapphire fire, acknowledging its mastery – then a chord on Jim's guitar released her, she levelled her head and looked out at what she knew was there, would hear in another heartbeat but would never see: the crowd. And, at the second chord, before Jim's voice came in, she began to dance, hesitantly, delicately, to the plangent sound that entranced her. Like a skirmish, and then a battle, and then Armageddon, the great animal applauded, striking together its thousands of palms, stamping with its thousands of feet, whistling and shrieking its approval. But she continued to dance, inventing steps as Jim repeated chords, until the crowd quieted and they could go on with their act.

Later, she sat alone in their dressing-room, wondering, or pretending to wonder, why Jim had not joined her as he usually did after the last performance. It had been a half-hour since she had bowed to the crowd and run past the bandstand, through the narrow corridor to the dingy room where they dressed. Jim should have followed her a few minutes later – he always sang one more song after she danced 'The Blue-Tail Fly'. But he had not come just as he had not come several nights that week. She had sat in front of the spotted mirror, a kimono thrown over her bare shoulders, buffing her finger-nails and waiting for him. She had smoked cigarette after cigarette, knocking the ashes on to the linoleum floor until there was a ring of grey smudges all around her chair. Still Jim did not come. Finally, she sighed and stood up, letting the kimono slip off her shoulders and fall in a silken wave to the floor. She glanced at her made-up face in the mirror, noting the dark circles that even Max Factor's make-up did not hide, then pawed at the cold cream and splashed it on her cheeks. Of course, she could go out and find him, as she had done the other night; he would be at the bar or at somebody's table. She did not mind that – if he were just at the bar or having a drink at some stranger's table – what she feared was that he would be at Vanessa's table. That was where he had been the other night. She had almost gone up to him, had come within an ace of speaking to him, before she had seen that the woman who was with him was the specialty dancer whose act preceded theirs. Then, as she stood there in the midst of the crowd on the verge of speaking his name, she remembered how on the first night of their engagement she had found him in the shadows of the bandstand watching Vanessa. She had seen the look in his eyes as the tall, auburn-haired woman did her ridiculous dance with the macaw – she danced nude except for a G-string, but she had trained the macaw to cling to her body as she posed and postured, clothing her obscenely with his great green wings and scarlet-and-yellow breast. Yet Vanessa had only one macaw, and it had been trained to cling to that part of her body which she displayed to the crowd; as she turned and pranced and the parrot preened, anyone in the bandstand or lurking near it could make out the secret places of her form in the clarity of the rose-coloured spotlight she favoured. As she had remembered this, she glanced at Jim, sitting across from Vanessa at the table, and she saw the same look in his eyes that had been there when he leaned against the bandstand and watched her pose with the parrot; her face had flushed with certainty, she had not spoken, but had turned and left the night club, had gone to their hotel room and to bed, lying awake half the night until Jim returned – but even then not telling him what she had seen, what she suspected.

She had no claim on him. This she knew, just as she had known earlier that year when she had given in to his advances, had run off from the conservatory without a word to anyone, had let him buy her the blue costume and teach her the dance, that it would not last, that she was only an episode to him, a silly schoolgirl who happened to have enough talent to work into the act. Knowing this, she had gone off with him anyway, partly because when he was near her, when his eyes held hers the way they had that first night at the bar when she had not been able to look away, she felt an excitement, a sense of being alive, of feeling herself and knowing herself to the fullest extent that she never had at any other time – but also partly because of her father, because of the rage he would fly into when he received the telegram from the school, because at night, when she lay beside Jim in the aura of his warmth, she thought of her father's impotent anger, his empty moralizing, and was sure that at last she had triumphed over him.

But, although she had known that some day this would happen, that the time would come when Jim would meet someone else and she would be faced with the choice of leaving him or staying with him and ignoring his infidelity, she had not yet allowed herself to reckon with the predicament. Nor did she now. Instead she rubbed at her coldcreamed face vigorously, threw the dirtied towel aside, pulled open the closet and squirmed into her dress without taking off her costume. She did not care if it did get wrinkled – let him worry about getting her another! Hadn't the whole affair been his idea in the first place? Hadn't it been he who had thought of the dance, who had insisted on the special costume, who had made her stay up night after night until she could do it with precision and professional polish? Well, if he wanted to throw her out, she didn't care. Let him teach that fat pig and her damn parrot to toe-dance – she was fed-up!

She shrugged herself into her coat and left by the back door to avoid seeing Jim. Outside, it was windy and cold and damp; August was ending in blustery weather. She burrowed her head into the gusty breeze and walked in the direction of the hotel, her skirts fluttering and the fine, misty rain wetting her face like tears. But before she reached the hotel the wind's cold fingers had investigated her legs and found the metalled cloth of her costume, her body had grown stiff and icy, her teeth were chattering. The blinking neon sign of an all-night lunchstand caught her eye, so she pushed open the door and walked into its steamy interior.

She had seated herself at the counter and ordered a cup of coffee before she realized that all the other customers were men of the roughest type. Next to her sat a great hulk with a bulbous nose, a thatch of reddish hair and protruding eyebrows; he was blowing on his soup and seemed to be oblivious of her. She looked the other way, and saw a small, shivering man with a face like an axe and watering eyes, one of which was lowering itself in an exaggerated wink. Her hands clutched the marble counter convulsively and she looked neither right nor left; even so she saw in the streaked mirror that all the rest of the men in the lunch room were staring at her. A cup of coffee slid in front of her, stopping abruptly as if it had reached the end of its tether, slopping a chicory-smelling, sticky liquid over the saucer and one of her hands. Its sudden appearance and its novel mode of locomotion startled her; despite her resolve not to look around, she did glance down the counter, and saw the dirty apron and silently heaving belly of the man to whom she had given her order – she even glimpsed his toothy grin.

Picking up the cup, separating it from its saucer and placing a paper napkin in the slop, she decided to take her time, to sip the hot, sugary stuff slowly, not to let the men frighten her. She had dealt with worse than them. In another town, and earlier in the summer, a man had followed her to her dressing-room, had pushed past the open door and stood silently behind her while she changed. Her first knowledge of his presence had been the awareness that someone else was breathing in the room. She had turned around and looked at him, had made no attempt to grab her clothes, had simply confronted his eyes with her own until he turned and fled. Jim had caught him outside the door and had cuffed him, but she had always regretted that this had occurred. She had handled him on her own, and Jim's action had been superfluous.

So she drank her coffee now, slowly and ostentatiously, and pretended not to hear the remarks that were passed. When she had finished, she lighted a cigarette and smoked it long enough to be convincing before she placed a nickel on the wet surface of the counter and walked to the door. But as she reached the street, as the cold wind struck her face and she once again felt the discomfort of the costume beneath her dress, she became less plucky. She had walked only a few steps down the street towards the hotel, when she heard the door bang shut behind her and she sensed that she was being followed. And when she heard a toneless, tuneless whistle, she knew that it was true.

She tried to take longer steps, to move her feet more rapidly, but the costume was too rigid. Perhaps it was better to maintain a steady pace so that whoever it was who was behind her would not know that she was frightened. Which one, she wondered, had made up his mind to accost her? It would not be the counterman, his very girth disqualified him, and he would have to stick with his job. The shifty-eyed one with the rheumy eyes and the sharp, rabbity face? She sincerely hoped not, although, if worst came to worst, he might be better than the lumpish one with the beetling brows and the rotten nose. The footsteps behind her sounded closer, they were all but running.

It was then that her clothes fell from her, dissolving away like spume in the surf. She stopped, ashamed and yet proud. The wind that had been cold now seemed warm and caressing. A great flush spread over her, tinting her flesh with the hue that typifies both embarrassment and the heights of ardour. The gauze wings, which she thought she had removed before putting on her dress, which she must have removed but which now amazingly appeared again just when all decent covering vanished, these wings began to shimmer ecstatically in the warm wind. They gave her a sense of power, a knowledge of freedom, and – instead of running madly on down the street – she turned to face whoever had been following her. It was her father.

Or rather it was not her father, but a faceless thing dressed in her father's clothes, the long-lapelled, black serge suit, the black velvet tie and rolled-brim black homburg, the tightly furled black umbrella. Where her father's sombre countenance should have been was an empty space, a hole in time, a whistling fissure. As the figure advanced towards her, she felt herself drawn towards it, and the sound that she had mistaken for a masher's whistle rose in volume and pitch, became a hellish lament. The wings at her shoulders at the same time gained weight and strength, they ceased quivering and began to beat; but just as she felt that she had the power to rise off the ground, to soar and escape her father, he was upon her. His long, black flags of arms shrouded her in a tenacious grasp – they reached for her beating wings, tore at them, sought to pinion them. She did not succeed in escaping him, but he failed to hold her down to earth: locked in hideous struggle, they both began to rise, and for an instant hung dizzyingly high in the air. Then the shrill sound of doom that issued from the abyss of his face mounted to a scream, a howl, quickly surpassing itself in volume, encompassing her in its violent clamour and, once more, she fell into the pit.

Around, up, on all sides and down, there was only blackness. She existed in a vast, frigid whirlpool of nothingness. Spinning with sickening celerity, she felt that she was disintegrating, that this vertigo that was now her only consciousness was the prelude to oblivion, destruction itself. She could no longer see, since all about her there was nothing but night; she could no longer hear, because the banshee cry stopped her ears. Her sole sensation was that of a horrendous, plunging oscillation; time's flow had frozen, became glacial, space

130

and the objects that had defined it had been swallowed by the vortex. Yet when she gave up, submitted to the frenzy, she saw light.

At first it was just a point, the merest pinprick of radiance, a splinter of brilliance. Still it grew, as she watched in hope and with a wild, hysterical joy, to a mote, and then a ray, and then a beam. It had the lustre of sunshine, the confident yellow warmth of morning. As it expanded, infusing the swirling night with first a glow and finally a blinding illumination, she felt herself breathe again, her pulse begin to beat and time's ice begin to melt, to trickle and ultimately to flow. Four walls settled down about her, and a ceiling – a surface marred with cracks, an enigmatic map of an undiscovered continent. Somewhere a child cried. Footsteps sounded near and yet far – they were in the hall, and she was lying in bed in a hotel room. But – and now she raised herself to another level of wakefulness – something had been happening, a spinning blackness, a sense of shame, her father. As she tried to remember, an image suddenly existed in her mind, an image of her own nudity, of a tall black figure standing near her reaching out for her, of a whirling blackness that fed upon her fear with the voracity of a beast. She sat up in bed, her eyes wide now, awake but still terrified by her nightmare. And as she stared at the door, a metal door varnished brown to look like wood, at the keyhole with its key and its dangling, red, fibre tag, she knew that she was in some place where she had never been before, and yet she knew that a terrible thing was happening again.

It could not be. She could not awaken twice like this, she could not die twice in that pit and yet survive, yet on surviving turn and look and find, twice – that! This time she would not turn, she would not look. She had been tricked, she had been dreaming about that old time (bit by bit it came back to her now), about that night, when she was a girl, that she had fought with Jim, when things had happened that even now she was uncertain had actually happened, that even today, this very moment as she sat up in this strange bed afraid to turn, afraid to look, she did not know whether she had dreamed them then, whether she dreamed them now.

And as she stared at the brown-varnished door that she was certain she had never seen before, even as she made sure in her own mind that *that*, at least, was real, she remembered Dr Danzer's words when, after the first of her 'treatments', she had recalled that confusing night, remembered wholly that terrible awakening. 'I want you to think about what you have told me,' he had said. 'I want you to note its equivocal nature. I want you to decide whether what you remember is a dream, an imagined re-enactment of an early childhood conflict, or whether it did actually occur. But I also want you to know that since you have told me, I have checked with the authorities of the city you mentioned, and they have no record of such a violent death that month, that summer, that year.' And it seemed to her that Dr Danzer was speaking to her, his words echoed so loudly in her ear. 'The guilt you feel is an imagined guilt. The crime you did is an imagined one. It is no less real for all that. To you it is even more reprehensible because you desire it deeply. In your mind, in your imagination, you have committed this crime against this man, have through him struck at your father. He is dead for you, but the guilt you feel is not for this imagined death – but for the real death that occurred that summer while you were away from home with this man, the natural death of your father. You have told me that he died of a heart attack, unattended – that they tried to reach you, but the conservatory did not know where you were, that all the dean could say was that you had not been at school for months and that he had understood that you had gone home. This is the guilt you feel: that you desired your father's death and that your father died because of your neglect. This is what you must face. Once you have faced it, I think you will discover that the other memory is but a distortion of this one, a punishment you have devised for yourself.'

She settled back in bed and shut her eyes again, reassured once more by Dr Danzer. He had told her many times that whenever she became confused, whenever there seemed to be a gap, when she had forgotten something that had happened and wanted to recover the memory of it, that all she had to do was to think back to the beginning of the chain of events, to recall each link and finger it in her mind until she came to the one that was missing. So she knew that this was what she must do now. First, she had to disentangle the truth of that August night from the dream of it – to the extent this was possible. For although she knew that Dr Danzer must be correct, that it only made sense of what she thought had occurred that night had actually never happened except in her imagination, she had never been able to dispel a modicum of doubt. Then there was the dream she had just had, which in many ways corresponded exactly to the reality of that summer and its climax, but which distorted other parts of it unnaturally. It was true that she had visited the Black Cat by herself, that she had met Jim Shad there but had not told him who she was until she had allowed him to make love to her. And it was also true that she had kept on seeing him without letting either Molly or Ann know what she was doing, that she had run away from the conservatory with him because she loved him and because she wished to be free. She knew it was a fact that he had taught her to dance and had used her in his act, had had a special costume made for her that fitted the name of a song he liked to sing. But, of course, in the dream she had just had these events, that had taken months to occur, had slipped into one another in a night, fitting together one inside the other like a Chinese puzzle. Still, it was true that Jim had taken up with Vanessa, that she had grown jealous of her, that one night when Jim failed to return to the dressing-room after the act she had flown into a rage and had decided to walk back to their hotel alone. She also remembered growing cold on the windy street and stopping at a lunchroom for a cup of coffee, and that when she had resumed her walk someone had been following her. But there the dream became fanciful, losing itself in a maze of symbols and a nightmare terror. And it was at just this point that she lost track of reality altogether. She knew that she had begun to run, that whoever it was that was following her – or whatever it was – had come closer and closer . . .

She shuddered and held herself stiff and rigid on the bed. Despite Dr Danzer's good advice, it did not work. She had reached the link but all she remembered was the substitute fancy, the thing that she knew had never happened, could not possibly have happened – had not Dr Danzer gone to the trouble of checking the records? – that could only be a figment of her neurosis. And yet it was the only reality for her. If that had not occurred, what had? But, worse than that, why could she not turn and look around *now*? What was she afraid of finding? Why was she afraid that what had never happened, what Dr Danzer assured could not possibly have happened except in her mind, had happened again?

She would feel better if she knew how she came to be in this strange hotel room that was so uncomfortably like the one in that other city many years ago. But, although she tried, she could not yet remember the events of the recent past, of last night and yesterday. The only way she would discover them, she had long since realized from experience, was to use the doctor's method, to finger the links of the chain of memory – even if one of them were vague and dubious, she could by-pass that one – to follow them up one by one until they led her to the present.

After that night she had been jealous of Jim and had run away from the night club; *after what had probably never happened the next morning* she had been terrified and had left the city, had taken a train to her home half-way across the country, had returned to her father's house to find a funeral wreath on the door. Her father had died of heart failure in the night only a few days before, a neighbour told her. They had tried to reach her, but the conservatory thought she had come home. After this shock she had stayed at home the rest of the waning summer until her father's affairs were settled. The book-store was sold, the house and all its furniture, even her piano, was sold, and she found that she had money and could travel. That fall she had not returned to the conservatory, but had gone to New York and applied to Madame Tedescu. She had played for Madame, a frail old lady with ash-white hair whose name was known on two continents, and Madame had accepted her for a pupil. Her life for the next ten years had consisted of music: three years with Madame in New York from nine to twelve each morning, from one to six each afternoon, each day in the year with no vacation and only Sundays off; two years in Rome, after she had won a prize, with a spirited Italian master of ancient instruments; and then five more years, with Madame again, all over the face of Europe, concertizing in Paris, Brussels, Vienna, Berlin, Naples, Moscow, London. And, finally, not so many years ago, her first concert in New York's Town Hall, the bouquets of roses and one particular corsage of brown orchids from a tall, blond man who was that season's sensation as a conductor – Basil.

The happy years had been next: their marriage and those idyllic weeks on a New England farm, days like butter with its white froth in the churn, their new house in New York, their friends, Madame Tedescu, the kind words of the critics. And then another summer had come, and with it the difficulty, the blackness that arose out of her harpsichord, even when she played her beloved Bach, and overcame her. That memory had haunted her, the things that went wrong, the little pieces of days that somehow got all mixed up or irretrievably lost, her wanderings. And then her sickness, the days and weeks when there was only blackness, the hospital, the latticed window and the view of the elms . . .

She had that much of it straight, she could think of it, put each link in its rightful place. Except for the early, black, lost weeks, she could remember every incident of her stay at the hospital, recall all the nights when she had fought against the past and emerged victorious. All the days of the last week, the day she left the hospital, the days she went shopping, the interview with Dr Danzer, the luncheon with Nancy and the afternoon at her studio with its terrifying episode – yes, all this fitted into place, even her meeting Jim Shad, the ride in the taxi, her escape, the woman descending the front steps of her house against the setting sun, the letter in the console table that was inexplicably missing . . . And now she remembered what had happened next. She had gone into the library and found Basil seated at the piano; she had stood looking at him, afraid to speak lest her words betray her thoughts. She had watched him play for many minutes and then had turned about and left the house. As she walked the streets, going towards the midtown section and a small French restaurant where she might have dinner quietly, she had thought of the queer squarish bag she had found in one of her drawers and of the vulgarly scented powder spilled on her dresser. While she sat by herself in the little restaurant, drinking a glass of claret, she had thought of the doctor's warning that her husband might have changed, and she remembered the way Nancy had hinted at the same thing during lunch. And she had grown frightened and sad, and had drunk a few too many glasses of claret.

Later, on an impulse, she had bought a newspaper and looked in the advertisements for the name of the night club where Jim Shad was singing. She knew that in view of what had happened that afternoon the last thing she should do was to go to where he worked; but she wanted badly to hear him sing again, she wanted to be part of the anonymous crowd, to be there near him and yet in no way connected. She had stopped in another bar and had one more drink, this one a martini, to gather up her courage, and then had hailed a taxi to take her downtown to his night club, a Village cellar.

Once inside the small, low-ceilinged room with bizarrely painted walls that seemed to converge on the minuscule bandstand and even more minute dance-floor, she could not escape. She had not realized that the place would be so intimate – in her mind she still imagined Jim Shad singing in the great barns that were Middle-Western dance-halls – nor that at ten-thirty at night there would be so few people there. The head waiter had shown her to a table near the dance-floor, and only when she insisted had he allowed her to seek a darker corner where she hoped she could not be seen as readily. But no sooner had she seated herself than she realized that out of the dozen people at the bar and at tables around the room were the two she did not want to see her – one of whom she would never have thought would be there – Jim Shad and Vanessa. Even worse, Shad, who sat facing her, had seen her, had apparently watched her discussion with the head waiter over where she should sit, was smiling at her over Vanessa's shoulder, winking at her to let her know that he knew she was there, that he wanted to see her and would be around as soon as he could get rid of Vanessa.

She had wanted to leave, but she had known it was useless. If she had gone, he would follow her. As it was, she was safest in the night club. When he did his act, she would call Basil and get him to come for her. Sooner or later she would have to tell Basil about this – although she feared that if she did it would give Basil the opportunity for which he was probably seeking to ask for a divorce – tonight was as good a time as any. But in the meantime she had known that she would have to deal with Shad.

She ordered a drink and kept her eyes averted. This stratagem was ineffective: although she did not look at him, she could feel his eyes persistently on her, could not keep the image of his face, his casual smile, from rising up before her, could not divert her thoughts from him. The waiter brought her a drink and a bowl of popcorn and pretzels; she drank the martini slowly, intent on each sip, took pretzel after pretzel, crumbling each one until she had an ant-hill of cracker meal built up on the tablecloth. The cellar filled slowly; she could hear the head waiter speak to each couple as they came down the stairs, and by listening closely to the sound of their feet on the hardwood floor she detected where they had been seated. The piano-player trundled his midget piano to her table, placing it so that it blocked her view of Jim and Vanessa – or the view she might have had if she had looked up; he played several pieces rather badly, but it was a relief to be able to raise her eyes for a time, and when he had finished she gave him money. The orchestra came in – a small combination made up of piano, double-bass, trumpet and drums – and began to play the classics in a modified Dixieland style; they played cleanly, and if her mind had not been on Jimmy she would probably have liked their music. Suddenly she realized that the club was packed with people. They seemed to have come all at once – she glanced at her watch and saw that it was nearly midnight. The orchestra's playing became freer, the solos grew longer and the improvisation more ingenious. She began to watch the trumpet-player, a lean reed of a man who seemed to have the shakes, but he kept to the beat and knew how to develop a melody. A few minutes later she was watching the drummer, and then the big, dark-coloured man who slapped the bull-fiddle. Casually, as if it were accidental, she let her eyes flick over to the table where she had seen Jim and Vanessa. The auburn-haired woman was gone, but Shad saw her look at him, and instantly rose to his feet. Her fingers rolled the stem of her glass back and forth and her lips trembled as she watched him thread his way to her table. Then he was standing over her, a dark shadow on the circle of white of her table-cloth, saying, 'May I?' Of course, she had nodded her head.

Jim had sat down opposite her without another word. He had turned around and signalled to the waiter, who immediately brought him a bourbon. He had thrown this down his throat, squinting as he had used to do as he did it, but making no comment. She said nothing. He took a handful of popcorn and began to roll it kernel after kernel at her tiny, crumbling tower of broken pretzels. By the time he had rolled the last bit of popcorn across the table the mound was demolished.

'I talked to the boss,' he said. He did not drawl.

She did not look at him and gave no sign that he had said anything.

'I don't have to sing tonight.'

She sipped at her drink and looked away from him at the orchestra.

'I thought we might go some place. It's been a long time, Ellen.'

His voice, his presence, moved her, was by turns comforting and stimulating. She did not trust herself to look at him, but it was becoming increasingly difficult to avoid his eyes.

'If you are worried about her, don't be. I've taken care of that.'

To her surprise, she realized that she believed him.

'You are the only one I have ever cared for, the only one who has ever mattered. I would have come to you sooner, but I didn't know how to approach you. You've made yourself somebody, Ellen – you are great. I don't know why I acted the way I did this afternoon. I guess it was the way you looked at me . . . you looked at me as if you were afraid of me.' His voice was quiet, hesitant – she had not heard him stammer before – sincere.

'Let me get your coat,' he was saying. 'I love you and I want to be with you.'

And she had nodded her head.

She opened her eyes again. She sat up in bed, but she kept her eyes fixed on the brown-varnished door. That was the way it had been. She had gone with him. They had walked in Washington Square and sat on a bench and necked like a couple of kids. She had wanted to ask him what had happened that night so long ago, she had wanted to find out if what she remembered was true . . . or if the doctor was right and she had only imagined it. But it had hardly seemed the time.

He had taken her to a small hotel nearby, a place where he knew the night clerk. The only room available was a small one without a bath. She had looked up at the ceiling. She remembered that she had noticed the crack in the plaster when the bellboy had shown them the room, except that it had looked worse in the bald glare of the electric light than it did now in the soft morning sunshine. Jim had bought a bottle, and they had had a couple of drinks – then she had turned out the lights and waited for him while he went down the hall.

That was all she could remember.

Still looking at the door, she threw back the covers and got out of bed. She had nothing on, and there was a dark stain on her hands, her breasts and her thighs. She held her breath and determined to be calm this time, to reason it all out before she did anything, so that she would be sure to remember.

She found Jim's body between the bed and the door. His face was scratched and his throat was mottled. A dark stem of blood had spouted from his mouth and grown a black bud along his chin; when she touched it, it flowered redly. His head, the top of it, had been flattened, and his hair was matted with dried blood. When she looked back to the bed, she saw that there was blood on one of the posts, that there were dark stains on the sheet and the mattress. There was no doubt that he was dead – although she felt for his pulse – and that he had been dead for a long time.

She dressed quickly, opened the door a crack and looked to see if anyone were about before going down the hall to wash her hands. She scrubbed the bowl to make sure that she left no stains, then peered into the hall again and returned to her room. Once back inside, she slowly and cautiously searched the room to be certain that she was not leaving evidence of her presence. She found a bobbypin, three curling hairs, one with a split-end, and her lipstick. She stood over Jim's body, looking at it, trying to remember. It was no use. She opened the window and stepped out on the fire-escape.

As she was easing the window down from outside, her hands slipping on the dusty glass, someone began to hammer on the door of the room. The sound frightened her more than the sight of Jim's body had; her hands fell away from the window, allowing it to fall to the sill with a loud, slamming sound. She shrank back from the window, colliding with the railing of the fire-escape, losing her balance for an instant, catching a dizzying glimpse of the street many storeys below. It was all she could do to keep from pitching off the iron stairs, and when she had regained her balance she was so weak that she sank down on her hands and knees.

In this position she looked through the window into the room once more – in time to see the door bulge, the flimsy bolt break and the key fly out of the lock, the door swing open. A tall, auburn-haired woman, her face grey with anxiety, lurched into the room. Her hands spread apart as she saw the body; she ran forward and collapsed at Jim's side. Ellen saw that she was Vanessa.

Slowly Ellen crept down the gritty iron stairs of the fire-escape. Not until she was within jumping distance of the alley did she stand erect; then she leaped the last ten feet and landed on the kerb. When she reached the street, she stood on the corner and hailed a taxi.

Vanessa must have followed them when they left the night club; she must have waited outside the hotel all night for them to reappear. When, out of jealousy, she had at last been forced to pound on the door, she must have expected to confront Ellen with Jimmy. She could not have known what she would actually discover.

Ellen sat forward in the cab and, as it turned the corner into Fifth Avenue, looked back at the hotel. She did not think that she had been seen.

5

She did not think that she had been seen. She had stood looking down at the pale stalk of her arm, the white flower of her hand and the glittering crystal of the wine-glass it held, watching the wine-blood pour out on the hearth. A sound, a rubbing of cloth on cloth, made her glance up and into the mirror, where she had met Basil's eyes gravely regarding her own, Basil's head slowly, slightly – so that no one else might see – shaking in disapproval, remonstrating with her. 'Wine is for drinking, Ellen,' he said.

She turned about and faced him, archly bringing the wine-glass back to her lips, pressing its cold edge against them, 'I know,' she said. 'I don't know why I had to do that. Truly, I don't.'

'You did not have to do it, Ellen. No one made you.'

She thought about this for a moment, considering each word of what he said, listening to the sound of each syllable in her mind. 'I know,' she said. 'I didn't have to. I just wanted to. I did it because I wanted to.'

He continued to look at her, without speaking, his eyes clouded with worry.

She smiled at him and held out the glass. 'Fetch me another glassful, please, Basil. I promise I shall drink this one.'

He took the glass from her hand, but he did not smile. He hesitated, seemed about to speak – she saw his lips move. But then he walked away towards the butler.

There was something pathetic about him, she decided as she watched him walk between the chatting couples. Perhaps it was the way he held her glass stiffly in front of him, as if it were a signal or a warning. Or it might be that she was watching him in the mirror, that his reflection diminished him, made him seem smaller, almost childlike. But whatever it was that caused her to pity him – if it were pity she felt and not just heightened sympathy – did not matter; what mattered was that this was the way she felt, this was the way it was, the way it had to be. She shut her eyes as she turned around swiftly, her long, full, black velvet skirts swirling and whispering. She felt for the diamond choker at her throat, the choker that Basil had given her earlier that evening as she sat backstage trembling, waiting for the time to come, waiting to walk out of the wings and into the brilliant space, to stand with her hand on the chill mahogany of her harpsichord, to close her eyes and bow to the great, many-faced beast. Basil had approached her from behind then, too; she had heard his knock on the door, heard her maid greet him, had seen his face swim out of the dim reaches of her mirror into the foreground. She had spoken to him, shutting her eyes then, too, because she had been afraid that she might read on his face evidence of the same fear that she felt; she had only opened them as she felt the hardness, the heaviness at her throat, as if a metalled hand had caressed her reassuringly – but she had opened them

146

to grandeur, to bright fire and glory, to Basil's smile. This time when she opened her eyes, having completed her manoeuvre, having faced about, she saw only the smoke-palled drawing-room, the confusion of bare arms and backs, of dark suits and white shirts and dresses of many colours – and the pinkly enamelled wrinkles of her hostess's face, poor, doddering Mrs Smythe.

A grey, fumbling wraith of a form surmounted by a small, puckered, shiny mask of a face, Mrs Smythe had already clawed at her hand, had caught it and clasped it between her own desiccated bunch of fingerbones. Now she was cooing. 'My darling, you were wonderful. Such tone! Such colour! True, true virtuosity!'

She smiled at Mrs Smythe, feeling the skin of her mouth stretch, feeling her lips part in the social gesture. Her other hand rooted at the hard stones that guarded her neck, clung there as a sparrow in a storm clings to its nest. To keep the smile up, to display an undaunted face to Mrs Smythe and the room, took all her strength: her shoulders sagged, something within herself emptied, ruthlessly flowed like water down a drain, like wine out of a glass. But just as she was sure that her knees were going to give, that she would in another moment fall forward, sink down, down, a spark of anger flickered in her mind, flickered and finding tinder blazed, grew into flame and warmed her. Damn you, damn you, she thought as she smiled more broadly at her hostess, what right have you to give parties, to know everyone who counts and have favours to bestow? You know nothing of music, of my world of sound, of what it means to set tones down in space and time so that they relate, so that you can build on them other tones, inject into them rhythm, give them weight and meaning, construct with them a reality. You know only people, people you can twist and turn and force to do your bidding; you care only for power. And that is why I am here, why Basil is here, and you know it. Yes, I know and you know that it had to be you who gave a reception in my honour after this, my first 'return' concert, otherwise you might have lost a little of that prestige that is so precious to you. And we both also know that I had to accept your invation, and Basil, too, because old Jeffry Upman always comes to your parties and you tell him what his opinion should be. Jeffry's opinion! Jeffry's fame as a critic! Your opinion and your power! But where, Mrs Smythe, where do you get your opinion? From the music, from the tiny scraps of my sound you heard tonight when you were not chattering with one or another of your friends? Ah, no, not from the music – you have never learned to listen to music. You form your notions in subtle ways, if you can be said to have notions at all. You like those musicians and composers who will do as you suggest, who will add to your fame, who will cluster around you and heed your beck and call. It is like a snowball, isn't it, Mrs Smythe? As it rolls downhill it grows larger and larger, and you can grow larger with it, just like all the other little flakes of snow, if you put yourself in its path and allow yourself to adhere. But if you avoid the oncoming snowball, if you resist it, you will be thrust aside to shiver alone, you will be ignored. Damn you, Mrs Smythe.

But, in fact, Mrs Smythe did not resemble a snowball as much as she did a ghost. Except for her face, with its palimpsest youthfulness, she was alarmingly insubstantial. She seemed a shadow in grey lace, a wreathed, two-dimensional shade. Her hands were pink bones, her feet animated shoes. Yet she inspired no compassion, she was not helpless, but a vituperative relic, an awe-inspiring totem, perhaps, that had been placed in your path by an enemy to bewitch you. And as she complimented you, as she smiled her wrinkles at you, she was measuring you, testing your loyalty, calculating your potential fame and its future worth to her.

'What a lovely dress, Mrs Smythe – and what a lovely party! And now you say kind things to me, as well. I'm really overwhelmed!' As she said these polite words, made this fitting response, she noticed with cold amazement that they proceeded in proper sequence, made sense and seemed to meet Mrs Smythe's approval. But you could never tell for certain what Mrs Smythe was thinking. Her eyes, like gems imbedded in a crackled glaze, gave no clues; her gestures were inconsistent with her intentions; those who knew her well averred that the chief source of her power, other than her wealth, lay in her inscrutability.

'I want you to meet a delightful young man,' she was saying, her prehensile hand clutching avidly at Ellen's aching wrist. Bobbing her head solemnly, she began to usher her through the crush, brushing past a painter and his mistress, a bevy of cherubic composers chortling at a boyish witticism, a stern-visaged sculptress who seemed to have been rough-hewn by her own hand out of alabaster, to a tall and gangling fellow, an adenoidal youth with a receding chin and a furtive hand that tried to secrete his faintly moustached mouth as they approached. But he saw that it was too late, that they were upon him, and his hand fell away embarrassedly, grabbed at his pocket and, missing that, fell limply at his side – she saw the crop of uncultivated hairs that littered his lip, too long to be a mistake in shaving, not dense enough to act as an adornment, too red to be ever anything but fatuous. 'Ferdinand,' Mrs Smythe was commanding, 'I know you have been wanting to meet our guest of honour, dear Ellen here. Ellen, this is Ferdinand Jaspers. I'm sure you two will get along famously.'

And Mrs Smythe went on to another solitary victim, standing agape across the room from Ellen and Ferdinand, barely having halted her inexorable progress to introduce them. Ferdinand, she could see, was not used to Mrs Smythe. A flush had started above his collar and would soon threaten his face. His hand flew up to his mouth, jerked there for an instant, then fell reluctantly back again. 'I – I enjoyed your recital, Mrs Purcell,' he said. 'I – I enjoyed it very much.'

'Thank you,' she said, knowing that she should say more, that it would be unkind not to help him by holding up her end of the unnecessary conversation, yet enjoying his uneasiness.

He wet his lips and, as if its action were controlled by a mechanism, his hand skittered up to his head, patted and smoothed his clay-coloured hair. She was amused to see a droplet of perspiration forming on his brow and, while she waited for him to speak again, she chose to speculate as to which side of his nose it would streak down eventually. Then the silence that had held only one youth's shame was broken by a voice that sounded from somewhere in the room, that belonged to some one person in the clutter, a voice she almost, but did not quite, recognize talking about something she did not want mentioned, that she had hoped had been forgotten. '. . . how could you have kept from hearing about it? It was in all the papers. The more sensational ones even printed pictures of them lying there together, dead. A towel was thrown over his body, of course, and she was fully dressed. But, even so, I don't think they should print such things. They said she killed him, you know. Oh, it was based on the time of their deaths – according to the medical examiner he died hours before she did. That was how it was, or so they said. She killed him, for jealousy or for some other reason, and then got to brooding over it. The night clerk said he had rented a room to a man and a woman. No, but then would you expect them to give their *right* names? Yes, she must have felt remorse . . . killed herself. My dear, I was so surprised that you hadn't heard of it . . . a sensation, nothing less than a sensation. Why, I had seen him just a night or two before . . . he was singing in the Village, you know . . .'

Ferdinand cleared his throat and she recovered herself. She realized that all the time she had been listening to the other conversation, afraid to turn around to see who was speaking, she must have been staring at the youth, staring blankly and fixedly; but he might have taken this for a steady inquiry, an indication of another kind of interest. Quickly, she lowered her eyes.

He coughed. 'I – I am a poet,' he said.

Why, oh why, she asked herself, had he told her that? What did his being a poet mean to her? She continued to stare at him, realizing full well that even if he had at first mistaken her glance for coquetry, he could not now – seeing his face tighten, his ridiculous attempt at a moustache quiver as he grew more aware of her hostility, sensed that her look was a weapon.

'I – I mean,' he said, 'that I've had a book published. A little book of verse.' And his hand, like an eager retriever after a bird, swept up to his lip and then swept down again.

But, although she did not avert her eyes, she was not listening to him. She had heard the voice again, the voice that sounded familiar, which she was sure that, if she could only stop to think, she would be able to place. Once more it had risen above the continuous murmuring of the crowd, had broken free of the mass sound, and in its escape had seemed to create an area of quiet, a silence within the general noise, in which it alone existed, which it alone commanded. 'As a matter of fact,' the voice was saying, 'I remember that I'd seen him even more recently than that. Yes, I'd not only heard him sing just a few nights before it happened, but he had been in my studio that very afternoon . . . Oh yes, I knew him well . . . why, he used to drop around all the time . . . Who was she? No one you'd know, my dear. Some dreadful person – a dancer I believe, I read some place that she had been a dancer; yes, I'm altogether sure she was a dancer . . . Why? Why do they ever? She loved him, I suppose. Isn't that always the reason? Her name? Why, I don't think I remember. I read it once . . . it was in all the papers, of course . . . but now I can't remember . . .'

She recognized the voice, knew all at once without question that it could belong to no one but Nancy. And with this knowledge she felt herself compelled to cross the room, to seek out the voice, to confront Nancy and prove to herself once again that she had nothing to fear. Nancy had sounded behind her and at some distance – she must be back towards the fireplace. Thinking this, she turned about blindly and began to push her way through the chatting throng. The youth was aghast, his face lost all colour – she saw this out of the corner of her eye as she brushed past the nearest couple. She felt sorry for him. But she could not bother to return to him, to apologize for leaving him. It was too important for her to find Nancy, to break into her conversation, to hear clearly every word she had to say.

She sensed that her impulsive progress through the densely peopled room was causing comment, she could feel others' eyes on her – but she did not care. Yet she did force herself to walk more slowly, to go out of her way rather than to press herself between a tall man and a robust woman who impeded her passage, to look for Nancy instead of locating her only by the sound of her voice. In fact, she even stood still momentarily, gazing about the great, glittering room, and was rewarded by the sight of the person she sought. Nancy leaned against the fireplace, her granite face contorted by her emphatic speech, her thick-fingered, peasant's hands gesturing broadly. She was relieved to see her, but she did not hesitate any longer. Instead, she pushed forward again, even more impulsively than before, blundering against a sofa, nearly upsetting the butler and his tray.

Nancy saw her approaching. She turned away from her companion, a pallid man with sleek hair and an intense expression, to cry, 'Ellen, darling, you were incomparable. It was really an occasion! But, Ellen – I'm so glad we saw you now – I think you can help us out. Ellen, tell me, do you remember meeting a man, a musician, a singer of folk ballads, very popular, in my studio last summer?'

She nodded to the pallid man, to whom she had not been introduced. Then she looked directly at Nancy's massive face. 'You don't mean Jim Shad?' Her breathing slowed as she waited for Nancy to react, to show any indication that she *knew*.

But Nancy's face did not change. 'That's right. Well, I remember his name, too. But, Ellen, for the life of me I can't remember the name of the woman – she was a dancer, a dreadful person – who killed him. You knew that he was murdered, didn't you? I thought everyone knew, that simply everyone must have read about it – it was such a sensation; she beat his head in, you know! – but Jack here tells me that he didn't know. You knew about it, didn't you, Ellen?'

She smiled, amused by Nancy's chatter. 'It was terrible. I read about it at the time. Did they ever find who did it?' She was proud of her own calmness, her inventiveness.

Nancy's eyes widened and she plainly showed her disbelief. 'But, darling, that's what I'm trying to tell you! This woman, what's-her-name, did it. She bashed his head in, then shot herself – although why she didn't use the gun on him I've never understood. Only I can't remember her name. I thought you might. She was a dancer.' Nancy seemed to have run down.

She looked at her closely, saw her leaning against the mantel, her slouched stance, made sure that her face was blank with curiosity – or was it malice? 'Although why she didn't use the gun on him I've never understood,' she had said. Had she meant that ironically? Was she using this means to let her know that she suspected her? The thought tortured her and made her want to avoid Nancy's eyes. But she knew that she dare not do this, that if Nancy did suspect her such an action would help to confirm her belief. She must brazen it out.

'I remember now. I do think I read something about a dancer. She killed him, didn't she? Did you know her?' She spoke harshly, jerkily.

Jack, who had been smoothing the marble of the mantel with his hand, looked at her in surprise. But Nancy, if she noticed, did not show that she was aware.

'That was it, Ellen. The desk clerk said they registered

together under assumed names the night before. Then they found them the next morning. Both of them were dead. She had killed him first, then shot herself. Don't you remember her name?'

She pressed her hand to her throat, felt the diamond choker, was reassured by its unyielding presence. 'I can't say that I do. I'm sorry, but I'm afraid I didn't follow the case. It must have happened just before Basil and I went away. We went to his cabin in the Catskills, don't you remember? I had to get away from everything so that I could practise, and Basil was deep in his scores. We didn't see a newspaper all summer. I'm afraid I missed all the gruesome details.'

Nancy smiled. 'Of course, you wouldn't. I had forgotten that you and Basil were away. Why, you must have left that same week! Oh, well, it doesn't matter. I only wish my memory wouldn't play such queer tricks on me.'

She could see now that she had been mistaken. Nancy had meant nothing by her question, had just been curious, gossipy, as was her nature. But now that her mind had started on that track, now that the special, dry-mouthed fear, the calm panic, had returned, she was forced to remember other details of that morning, that morning that seemed years ago but was only months, that morning that she had returned to the house to find Basil sitting up in his leather chair in the library, sitting stiffly with his head twisted uncomfortably, asleep. She had known at once that he had waited up for her, that he must have been concerned about her absence. She had gone over to him and knelt beside him, had awakened him with a kiss.

His eyes had opened heavily, slowly, his hand had flown to his forehead and rubbed it, before he saw her and accepted the fact that, at last, she was there. He had hunched forward in his chair, feeling in his bones the cramps of an uncomfortable night – he had taken her hand between his own and pressed it tightly. 'Are you all right?' he had asked.

She had been far from being all right. She had been frightened and sick and on the point of killing herself. On the way uptown in the taxi Shad's face had haunted her, and even at that moment she could sense the blood upon her body like a weight or a burning brand. But she had not known how to speak to him of this. She had known that something within her was wrong, badly wrong, that in some way she was both wrong and bad. Yet the pressure of his hands on her own gave her strength, enabled her to lie. 'I'm quite all right,' she had said.

Later, much later, she had decided to tell him nothing about it. She had been clear in her own mind about that. He would learn of it soon enough, she had reasoned, from others – more brusquely perhaps, but less emotionally, than if she had tried to tell him. She had gone to her study, had locked the door, and for the first time since she had returned from the hospital she had addressed herself to her instrument. It had been all that day as if her fingers, her body – yes, even her mind – had not belonged to her; as if, so she remembered it, the hesitant music she made had not been heard by her, as if even her breathing were not her own. She had felt herself to be an instrument, a cruel, polished edge of surgical steel, lying on a sterile cloth, whetted for use. And the music, the sounds her fingers brought into being, had been bright, sharp slivers of tone that had lacerated the silence.

At dusk Basil had knocked at the door and had

persuaded her to come to dinner. Later, because he had wanted to and it had not displeased her, they had gone for a walk. He had bought a newspaper at the entrance to the park and they had gone inside, had sat on a bench to read it. If she closed her eyes even today (although she dare not close her eyes now with Nancy looking at her) she would still be able to see that headline, vaguely black in the indirect light of the lamp-post, that had told about Jim Shad's murder and Vanessa's suicide. She had reached for the paper, had torn it from Basil's hands, had read the entire story. At first she could not understand why Vanessa had killed herself, and then she realized that the police did not understand either. It had seemed comic to her that the police should think that Vanessa had killed him; she had wanted to laugh, to sob, to get up and dance like a child in pigtails, but she had known that if she had she could never have explained her action to Basil. As it was, he had wanted to know why she was so interested in the murder. 'This paper features a murder every night,' he had said. But that had been easy enough. She had told him that she had met Jim Shad only yesterday at, of all places, his sister's, Nancy's, studio. She had said that it was the first time that a friend of hers had been murdered and that she was naturally interested.

But a few days after that night, when Basil suggested that they go to the Catskills, she had been relieved at the prospect of leaving the city, of being alone, cut off from everyone, so she could think it through. Of course, Basil was with her most of the time – except for two weeks in August when he had conducting dates at several summer concerts. Being with Basil had been different, though, had been almost the same as being alone, they had been a part of each other. Her

157

harpsichord and Basil's piano had been transported to the cabin, and they split the days between themselves: in the morning she practised and he did what he liked, in the afternoon Basil read manuscripts and played critical passages while she went up the mountain sides in search of laurel or found a brook in which she could splash and wade. At night they had been together, driving along the twisting mountain lanes or lying back on the dewy grass, their eyes on the stars, their arms about each other.

She had never thought it through. She had made several false starts. One time she had decided that she would go to Dr Danzer, whom she was supposed to have called but had not, and tell him everything. On another occasion she had decided that this would be useless, that Dr Danzer would say what he had said before. He would tell her that this had not happened, that it was an hallucination, a figment of her neurosis that arose out of another, older guilt. But she had believed this for only a little time. Then the other aspect of her self, the sceptical part of her, had scoffed. She knew that whatever had happened that last night with Shad, had happened; it was real. It had not been a dream. Shad was dead, and his death had been recorded in the newspapers. What was more – and the strange thing was that she could formulate the thought, could think of it coldly as a fact, without alarm – it was more than likely, it was probable, that she had killed him.

'I've always said that there was something in the case that never came to light.' Nancy's remark sounded like a trumpet to her ears. Abruptly, her reverie was shattered, and she became electrically aware of Nancy and the danger of her chatting tongue. 'The police said this woman was jealous of him. They found witnesses who had seen them quarrelling, who had heard her accuse him of infidelity only the night before she killed him. But they never mentioned who she was jealous of, never a word leaked out as to who it was he was carrying on with – they made a real mystery of that!' Nancy tossed her head to emphasize her point. Jack, her pallid companion, nodded his perfunctorily – he was plainly bored with the conversation.

She could not decide whether Nancy actually suspected anything or not. But she did seem to keep coming closer and closer to the truth – if she were really clever, this might be a test. 'Oh, I think the police knew!' she exclaimed, trying to make her voice seem exasperated, as if she were tired of talking about an old, sordid crime. 'They undoubtedly questioned the person, found she was innocent and didn't release her name. Would you want to see an innocent woman's reputation ruined?'

Nancy looked at her closely and smiled slightly. 'Why, Ellen,' she said, 'what a horror you must think I am! Of course, I shouldn't want to see this mysterious person's name in print. I'd just like to know who she was, that's all. You see, Jim Shad was my friend. I can't help but be curious, and I should think you would be. Didn't you meet him at my house the very day before he was murdered?'

She opened her mouth to speak, to say something, anything, to keep off the silence and allow herself time to think. But before she could speak, Mrs Smythe, wraith-like, materialized at her side. Her brittle fingers clung to her elbow, her wrinkled face smiled coaxingly. 'Darling Ellen, I am loath to tear you away from these charming people, but dear Jeffry is waiting to see you. He attended your concert, you know, and he is going to do a little piece about it in tomorrow's paper. But, darling, he wants to see you first; he wants to have a little discussion, and he has a deadline to meet. So I'm sure your kind friends will excuse you!'

The birdlike pressure on her arm was surprisingly forceful; she found herself swivelled about by Mrs Smythe and obliquely propelled through the crowd to another part of the room where Jeffry Upman sat, alone and gingerly, upon a gilt chair, tapping at the darker squares of the parquet floor with the ferrule of his tightly-rolled umbrella. He was a thin, palsied, old man whose slight figure was bent into the shape of a question-mark. Whether his bodily posture had anything to do with his aesthetic predilection for the rhetorical question had long been a moot point among the wags of Fifty-seventh Street; however, all his reviews were spotted with indications of interrogation like raisins in bread-pudding. 'Last night in the august halls of Carnegie,' he would write, 'among the accustomed pomps and amid the proper hush, Mr Blizz-Blazz revealed himself to be one of the consummate artists of our time. There was something in his tone that melted, although it at no time lacked the vertebraic rhythm of authority, something that commanded our most subtle emotions and demanded a quality of listener on a level with the quality of Mr Blizz-Blazz's musicianship. Were there some in the audience who noticed, on occasion, a slight divagation from true pitch? Did others seem to feel that, here and there, inflections could be descried that were untraditional, if not debatable? Perhaps, one or more in the audience were aware of certain inconsistencies of tempi, of an unfortunate tremolo, some ill-chosen retardations? If so, these connoisseurs were the exception, as the cataclysmatic applause that greeted the artist after his second number spontaneously attested

160

to the circumstance that unequivocal recognition and enthusiastic approval were Mr Blizz-Blazz's due. Later, the programme promised that this unparalleled artist would return to play concertos by Mendelssohn, Tschaikovsky and Sibelius, as well as smaller pieces by Lalo, Debussy and Thomson; but, unfortunately, the lateness of the hour and the excruciating length of modern programmes prevented our further attendance.'

Jeffry had been a music critic in New York since before the days of Gustav Mahler; he was now not only super-annuated, but somnolent, a fact that more than one concert-goer had discovered for himself by glimpsing him drowsing in his seat through the most thunderous of symphonies. Usually he contrived to stay awake through the first number or two, but after that sleep overcame him. To many musicians sleeping critics are not too different from sleeping dogs, and Jeffry's sleepiness might not have become an object of jest if he had not also been inclined to snore. More than one violinist, while playing an unaccompanied suite of Bach's or the quiet movement of a Debussy sonata, had become uncomfortably aware of Jeffry's unintended, but frequently disastrous, obbligato. Curiously, his reputation did not seem to suffer from his habit of catnapping in concert halls; some said this was because of Mrs Smythe's influence, and it did play a part, but it was more probably just another manifestation of our society's respect for anything that is old and accustomed. People were used to seeing Jeffry Upman's signature in the papers, a decade or more ago he had written several books on 'music appreciation' that Mrs Smythe had connived to have distributed by a book club, and to the general public he was as much a fixture, a respectable piece of cultural furniture, as

161

an ageing statesman – most people do not read music criticism anyway.

She knew all these things, and she realized that it was useless to feel bitter towards senility. Even so, as she stood before him and saw his trembling head, his dull, heavy-lidded eyes and his pale, blue-veined, old man's flesh, she felt a desire to laugh at him, to pull him off the gilt chair and onto his feet, to turn him about and display him to the party, to cry out, 'Here you are! Look at him. This is what passes on the music you hear, this is the person whose review you will read tomorrow to find out if what you heard tonight was good or not!' But, of course, she did not do it.

Her presence was a formality, as was his. They both knew it, and showed that they knew it to each other as they fumbled for words. Mrs Smythe broke the silence. 'I was sure, Jeffry, that you would want to speak to dear Ellen. Everyone, *simply everyone*, was amazed at her brilliance tonight.' These were Jeffry's instructions, for which he had been waiting, she knew. And she also realized that Mrs Smythe had forced the encounter, that Jeffry had not been 'eager to see her', but only waiting to discover what his friend's verdict would be.

How Mrs Smythe arrived at her verdict no one knew – least of all Jeffry. But it was not irrevocable, and she would have to play the game out, to be polite to the thin, old figure who questioningly tapped with his umbrella as he peered up at her, whose eyes were already all but shut, who wanted nothing better than to get out of this hot, noisy room, away from all these milling people, so that once more he might fall asleep.

'It was most kind of you to come, Mr Upman,' she said (what else was there to say?), 'I am looking forward to reading your notice.'

Jeffry jiggled a bit on his chair, and the umbrella tapped more loudly. He coughed, drily, once, twice. She remembered that he always prefaced his remarks with this ritual. When he spoke, his voice sounded like a piece of chalk drawn across a blackboard or an out-of-tune piccolo. 'Splendid! Splendid! Splendid!' he squeaked. Then he looked down at his hand and watched it travel to his vest, cautiously observed it as it plucked a gold turnip from his pocket and snapped the lid to reveal two spidery hands converging on an ivory dial. 'Splendid!' he wheezed as he stood up gradually, his knees stiff, his body bent, his feet the dot of the question-mark. 'It's late. I must go.'

'Jeffry, you can't,' Mrs Smyth said firmly and, as he continued to stand, showed that she meant what she said by pushing him down again on to the fragile chair. 'Ellen has promised to play for us, and I know you will want to listen.'

The old man's chin sagged and his lips trembled querulously. But all he said was, 'Splendid! In that case. By all means. Splendid!'

The conversation, if it could be called that, ended as peremptorily as it had been begun by Mrs Smythe's inexorable pressure on her elbow. Meekly, she turned away from Jeffry and allowed herself to be urged by her persistent hostess into the crowd of guests. This time she was directed towards the far end of the great room, towards a raised platform that was decorated with velvet drapes and bedecked with two tall vases of roses and upon which sat the harpsichord Mrs Smythe had foresightedly provided for the occasion. Throughout the evening the drapes had been drawn, the instrument concealed, and even now the butler was still occupied with tying back a flounce, adjusting the position of the rose-filled vases. As they proceeded among the guests, they became gradually the centre of attention. What signal had Mrs Smythe given to invoke this miracle, this sudden, unexpected quieting of talk, this concentrated curiosity? Perhaps none, or perhaps the butler had been instructed to open the drapes when he saw them talking to old Jeffry, or, most likely yet, the entire evening had been planned to conform to a strict time schedule. Whatever her method, the fact remained that Mrs Smythe's receptions always featured these swift, appropriate changes-of-scene, always betrayed the presence of an experienced stage director, no doubt Mrs Smythe herself.

As she thought this, she caught sight of a diminutive person, a slight bowed figure in watered silk – Madame Tedescu. She was standing a little to the left of a group of two men and a vivacious woman that they were to skirt. Forgetting Mrs Smythe, she swerved in the other direction and pushed her way to the smiling old lady whose solitary presence meant so much to her. Madame Tedescu was in her sixties, her face had shrunk with age and weakness required that she lean upon a gold-headed ebony cane. Her hair was white and fell softly upon her shoulders, but her eyes were as bright and her smile as witty as the first day Ellen had come to her studio.

Madame saw her coming. The smile widened and her eyes glistened. She remembered that Madame had many times earnestly told her that she was her favourite pupil, 'the only one to whom I wish to entrust my tradition'. Knowing this, she also knew that Madame would not lie to her, that Madame would tell her sincerely whether she had played well tonight.

Mrs Smythe, surprised at her escape, caught up with

her just as she reached her old friend and teacher. As if she sensed that Ellen had a particular reason for breaking away, she managed to place herself between them and to speak first. 'You should be very proud of our Ellen tonight, Madame. Dear Jeffry was telling me only a moment ago that this recital was one of the great events of his lifetime. Of course, you will read his piece tomorrow to find out all he says, but I can tell you now, confidently, that it will be a paean.'

She had thought that she was accustomed to Mrs Smythe's rudeness and her arbitrary statements, but she had also thought that even Mrs Smythe would not be so crass. If she blushed, if she felt her throat go dry, it was not only out of embarrassment, but because she quickly realized that one reason why Mrs Smythe had not wanted her to see her old friend, and why she was now attempting to influence her opinion as she had Jeffry's, might be that even Mrs Smythe, whose taste in music was appalling in its absence, had known that tonight something had been wrong.

'You do not need to tell me about Ellen.' Madame Tedescu spoke slowly and with still a trace of a Viennese accent. 'I was at the concert. I listened.' She nodded her head solemnly, but then she looked at her and smiled. Her eyes were grave and her smile was kind, but by means of a simple change of expression, an admission of melancholy, she conveyed to her that she was concerned. 'I have not seen you in years, Ellen,' she said, but there was no reproach in her voice. 'Could you come to my studio tomorrow? Some time in the morning would be best. We can talk better there.' And, still smiling, she reached out and stroked her shoulder.

The butler had finished with the drapes and the vases – Mrs Smythe was eager to manoeuvre her prize on to the stage. 'Ellen has consented to play for us, Madame. In just a few minutes.' She shifted her feet restlessly, the grey veils of her frock moving mysteriously, as if to imply a haste she was too polite to mention.

Madame Tedescu stopped smiling, and her expression became wholly serious. 'But you are tired, aren't you, Ellen? You have played enough tonight.' Her tone seemed a little severe.

Mrs Smythe showed her presence of mind. She turned about instantly, her manner sympathetic, but her voice firm. 'I shouldn't want you to play if you are too tired, Ellen darling,' she said. 'I am only too aware of how exhausting your concerts must be! But, darling, Jeffry will be so disappointed!'

Although she did not want to play, although she wanted only to leave this absurd reception, this roomful of outrageous people, to get out of doors and feel the wind on her face, to look up and see the dark sky, to be alone, she understood the threat in her hostess's words, knew that if she did not comply with her wishes and play, Mrs Smythe was capable of speaking to Jeffry again, of changing her verdict and his. And she was afraid, not as much from what Madame had said as from her manner, that she would need Jeffry's little 'paean' tomorrow.

'Of course I'll play,' she said to Mrs Smythe. And to her old friend, pressing her hand, 'You'll see I'm really not too tired. And I promise to visit you in the morning.'

Madame Tedescu was not displeased at her decision, although her nod of acknowledgement was brief and her smile wry. But Mrs Smythe was fairly tugging at her arm, and she knew her reluctance would become

166

obvious if she lingered any longer. So she allowed herself to be led to the platform.

While her hostess raised her voice to announce that she had consented to play, she seated herself at the strange instrument and closed her eyes. In a few moments she would have to place her fingers on the manuals, to arch them and strike notes, to cease thinking about the world of herself and to think only of her world of sound. Or that was the way it should be. It had not been that way, except on a few, scattered occasions, for a very long time. Since the early part of the summer, since the week she left the hospital, she had played some part of every day. Her fingers had played, the notes had sounded as her eyes had read the page or her memory had prompted her. All the old tricks had returned, her virtuosity was if anything greater than it had ever been. But only a few times had it been *right*. Almost invariably all the sounds had been there and in the proper places, the tone had been accurate, the phrasing exactly what she wished it to be. Still it seemed to her that her playing had remained but a procession of sounds, an alternation of tones, a ragbag of phrases. There was no whole; it worked, when it worked at all, in fits and starts, inanely. Yet her technique remained impeccable, her fingers responded to her mind's demands, all the notes were there. If it were her world no longer, if it had ceased to make sense to her – and, truly, it had – where was her fault, what had gone wrong?

Mrs Smythe had concluded her announcement, and now a ripple of applause informed her that they were waiting for her to begin. She opened her eyes and looked at them, at their polished pink faces, their flushed bare arms and backs, their shining white shirt-fronts and flowing dresses, thinking how much they looked like a stiff prosaic collection of porcelain figurines adorning a bric-à-brac shelf. A pattern of sound formed in her head, etched itself precisely, making her feel alive and well: the first measures of Anna Magdalena's aria. If she could only play it once more the way she heard it! For Madame was listening, would be listening with all her intelligence, and if it came out right and good the way it used to come, she would know it and tell her. She looked for Madame among the pink faces, her eyes roving back and forth across the crowded room. She saw Jeffry, and over there was Nancy, still talking to the pallid man. Near them was a striking auburn-haired girl, a beautiful girl in a lustrous black gown, a girl who was familiar. She was talking to a blond man, talking seriously, quietly, as if she loved him. Who was the man? He looked familiar, too; but, then, she could see only part of him – the rear of his head, his shoulder and his hand raised in a gesture that she was certain she knew, that she surely had seen many times before. The girl stood partly in front of him, turned sidewise to face him, obscuring him from her view. Oh, now they were moving! He had put his arm around her; they were walking towards an alcove, a darker corner, where they would not be seen. They were in love – she was pleased that she had seen them, that her eyes had alighted on them just before she struck the first chord; it was a good sign. But who were they? – why did she feel she knew them? She watched them as they worked their way arm-in-arm back to the alcove, watched them enter, and then saw the man's face for the first time as he pulled at the velour drape. He was Basil.

Her hand fell heavily on the manual, and the other followed mechanically. Her eyes settled upon the maze of black-and-white strips, stared fixedly at the two lean, naked rats that scampered back and forth in it in a blind endeavour to run out. She heard laughter, after a few minutes, and excited talk – but she could not take her eyes off the rats and their intricate game in the black-and-white maze. There was a sound, too, a sound of a glass falling, of brittle blood flowing, tinkling, of a thousand glasses breaking, a million drops of blood tinkling. But this sound mingled with the other sound, the laughter and the whispering; it had nothing to do with the poor naked rats and their frightening maze . . .

Then, for no reason at all, the rats stopped running, the maze reassembled itself before her eyes. Someone, somewhere, was clapping, a lonely sound. She looked down at her lap, and saw that the rats had nestled there, had fallen asleep like children after a hard run. The tinkling sound, the noise of a glass breaking, of blood flowing, persisted in her head, but now she recognized it as a melody, a very familiar tune that she had hoped never to hear again, a folk-song that she had just played:

> Jimmy crack corn, and I don't care!
> My massa's gone away . . .

6

'Jimmy crack corn! Jimmy crack corn!' The words stole
into her consciousness, were placed there as a placard
is placed in a shop window, obtruded from her sleep
like a finger of guilt pointing out her sin – lingered for
a long moment, echoing as the scream she had heard in
her dream still echoed, then lapsed into silence like a
stone dropped into a pool. She lay on the bed, very still,
hushed and quiet, tense. If only she did not remember! –
if only, this one night, she would not have to experience
it all again! By an effort of will she opened her eyes, let
her consciousness advance into the shadow world of
her room, strove to see forms instead of the swirling
darkness that held her prisoner on every side. That
darkness, that fearsome blackness, was, she knew, a part
of her dream; the darkness of the room was different,
as she would see if she could but keep her eyes open
long enough to accustom them to the small amount of
checkered light that filtered through the window. That
darkness belonged to a night long ago, and to another
night even before that – she only dreamed it now. Say it!
Say it aloud! If you can hear yourself speak it, you will

know it is true and you will not have to live through that night, those nights, again. Speak it! Say those words! Louder! Louder! *'I am not afraid of the dark. I only dream the dark. It is not here now, it is only there then, when I dream. I am not afraid of the dark!'*

Her voice sounded naked, alone and mad. It was not her voice, but a child's voice, shrill and whining. And she was afraid, terribly afraid, of the dark. It was here now, just as it had been there then in her dream. The dark surrounded her, a great, noisome, evil cloak that smothered her. There was no light anywhere, no alleviation, only shadow devoured by shadow, umbra and penumbra. Worse than that, there was distance and time, a great pit into which she must fall, on whose edge she trembled at this instant. Many times had she fallen into it, many times had she taken that awful plunge, that dizzying descent that was one prolonged, headlong flight down to the depths of the past, to another place, another era. And it had always begun like this, with that sudden wakefulness, those words in her ears, that echo of a scream. Then, gently, the edge of the pit began to crumble. She found herself scrabbling desperately for a handhold in the drifting, shifting, rapidly disintegrating earth. The scream that had been silenced so long was heard again, now a mere thread of sound – it existed in the pit and she was slipping towards it. She fought bravely, trying to crawl back, struggling like a dog in quicksand against the insubstantial ground, the encompassing shadows, the ruthless attraction of the abyss . . .

It was over this time as suddenly, as amazingly as it had been each time before. There was a flash, an explosion – if one could call it either of those things – of absolute dark, a sudden violence of black that was the null itself. In this she ceased to exist, lost all sense of self, of being, of knowing, merged inextricably with this mirror of nothingness . . . Yet this, too, passed, and she sensed again, saw light again, was seated in the park with the sun on her back, with green, green grass and blue, blue sky, and children.

She was sitting on the bench watching a squirrel eat the nut she had just given him. He was a clever fellow: he held the bulky nut firmly between his claws and nibbled at it industriously with his sharp, rodent teeth; but all the time that he seemed preoccupied with his task, his beady eyes, glittering targets of sight, were upon her, calculating, determining whether to run and hide the nut or to eat it here, whether there would be more to come or if this were all. The sight of him reassured her – he was alive, intelligent, amoral, her kin. This squirrel had his nut, and she had her life, or this present moment of it, at least. They both clung to it, ravened at it, and kept a keen lookout for transforming possibilities into realities. She laughed and the squirrel took alarm, popping his nut into his cheek and running to the nearest tree and up its trunk a foot or more, then freezing on the bark, blending with it, his head cocked, his eyes gleaming, still watching her. She laughed again, experimentally, but this time he did not move. She was quiet, and, after a few minutes of caution, he returned, slowly and circuitously, sat up and looked at her, demanding a relative's due: another nut.

It was the last in her bag, but she gave it to him, crumpling the bag up afterwards and letting it drop at her feet, where the wind caught it and carried it erratically down the slope, then dropped it, let it lie, like a drunken cat playing with a lame mouse. The squirrel eyed the crumpled ball of paper contemptuously, but made no movement in its direction. He knows that there are no nuts in it, she had thought, that if there had been I would not have thrown it away. And he will leave me soon to search for other sources of nuts, other people with other bags. But what about me? Where shall I go now? What shall I do?

She had stood up and began to walk down the path towards the zoo. It was silly to compare herself with a squirrel, silly and melodramatic. She patted the folded newspaper she carried under her arm. She was a person of note, a musician who had given a successful concert only last night. The proof of it was here – she patted the newspaper again – in the words of Jeffry's review, ' . . . a genuine experience . . . she reveals a bright, shining world of pristine sound.' The image of old Jeffry came into her mind, flickered before her eyes, obscuring momentarily the sunshine, the trees and the children. She saw the old man as she had seen him the previous night, sitting precariously on the gilt chair, tapping nervously with his umbrella at the polished floor. She heard him squeak, 'Splendid! Splendid!' But anger overcame her, she blinked her eyes and destroyed her sight of the old critic and, to make the destruction complete, she tore the newspaper out from under her arm and threw it in front of her on the path, taking pleasure in walking on it, trampling on it, rejecting Jeffry's lies. For what Jeffry had said, all his blessed euphemisms, his rhetoric and his allusions, had no relation to the truth. She knew what the truth about last night was: she had given a mediocre performance, she had not played as she had wanted to play, as she had been able to play in the past. She was no longer an artist.

Madame Tedescu had told her this frankly, although

she had waited for her to ask. She had gone to her studio that morning as she had promised – she had left it only an hour ago. The doorbell of Madame's great, rambling flat near the Hudson River had tinkled enthusiastically when she had pressed it, and before she could press it again and hear once more its tiny clamour, Madame had opened the door itself. The old woman had seemed smaller in her cavernous studio, more like a fragile marionette than a real person. She was dwarfed by her paintings – a huge Léger, a long, narrow Dufy, a massive Rouault – and even by her instruments: the two concert grands, the clavichord, the virginal and the rare harpsichord of intricately carved ebony that was supposed to have been Mozart's. They had sat upon an Empire divan in the farthest room, a high-ceilinged, cathedral-like studio whose many-paned windows overlooked the wharves where liners docked and the travellers sailed for the ports of the world.

At first Madame had asked her the usual questions about her health. They had talked about mutual friends and experiences and had gossiped about the musical world of New York and the Continent, about the strange tricks war had played with the lives of peaceful musicians, the political ones and the victims, the current successes and those to whom music was art, was life itself, whom the larger public habitually ignored. But after a time a natural pause grew into a lengthy silence.

Madame had regarded her, looked at her as she had when she had been her pupil. Her calm, grey eyes had been quietly speculative, her face composed and kind but intent upon its purpose. 'Now tell me about yourself, Ellen,' she had said.

She had looked away at the window, had gazed at

the splattered, reflected light of waves until it dazzled her eyes, and when she looked back again at her old friend she saw a blurred face, an indistinct smile. 'I have been working steadily,' she said, and looked down at her fretting hands. 'My technique is sound. My fingers go where I want them to go. When I look at a score, I hear it the way it should sound – as I have always heard it. I am all right.'

Madame nodded her head, but her eyes remained steadfast and did not seem to share in the gesture of agreement. 'I heard you last night. I know you have regained your technique. But that is not what I wanted to know.' She hesitated and seemed to think about what she was going to say next. Then she wet her lips and began again. 'Ellen, there is more to your life than music. There is Basil. There are the other things you do. Tell me about them.'

'Basil is very well. His new concert series is doing nicely. I'm sure you read the notices in the newspapers. Basil's career is assured.'

This time the old woman shook her head briefly, but vigorously. 'I am not asking about Basil's career – or yours. I know all I need to know about both of your careers. I want to know about you – about you and Basil.'

How could she tell her what she did not know herself? She could say that as a husband Basil was kind, considerate, attentive, occasionally distracted and not as concerned with her interests as his own. The letter in the console table, the powder spilled in the drawer, her glimpse of a girl leaving their house burnished by the setting sun – she could mention these facts, too. But what were they? – only impressions, unconfirmed suspicions. She could tell her about their summer in the

Catskills, the slow, peaceful days and the long, ecstatic nights. And she could also tell her about the two times during the summer when Basil had been away, the time he was called to the city on business and had been discomfited when she had asked if she might go with him – she had not insisted and he had gone alone, had stayed away several nights – and the two weeks of concert engagements. What about last night? Should she tell Madame the real reason why she had forgotten herself and had played a popular folksong instead of the Bach aria at the reception? What would Madame say if she described to her the beauty of the girl with the auburn hair and told her that she had seen Basil with her, kissing her? But it was nonsensical to think of it – she could not tell her any of these things. Instead, she said deliberately, a little too emphatically, 'Basil has been very kind.'

Madame again shook her head. 'Husbands can be kind, Ellen – and they can be unkind. I do not think it matters. What matters is whether he makes you happy. That is what I want to know.'

At last she could speak, say words that held meaning. 'No,' she said, 'I am not happy with him.'

'What is wrong?' Madame was inexorable. She sat with her hands clasped, her smile patient and just and firm.

'He has not been the same since – since I returned. Oh, he does everything he should. And he worries about me. For a while, last summer, we were happy. We were a part of each other and it was good. But then something happened.'

'Can you tell me about it?'

She shook her head. 'There is nothing I can tell you. Basil seems to withdraw, to be apart from me.

It's as if he tolerates me, and does not want me to come near.'

'Have you ever spoken to him about this?'

'No, I haven't. I know that it may be that I imagine it. I imagine too many things, you know. In the past, I have often thought that people were doing things to me when they were not. I have learned not to talk about my fears, to keep them to myself.'

Madame moved to her side and took her hand, pressed it between her own. 'You must talk to him about it, Ellen. I am sure you must. If you don't it will grow in your mind, this fear – it will destroy your life together. If there is something wrong, it will do no harm – it can only do good – to speak openly about it, to discuss it with each other. And if there is nothing wrong, if you are only imagining that he does not love you, you will learn that you are wrong. He will know about your fears and help you to face them. But, if he doesn't know . . . ?'

Madame stood up and walked to the ebony harpsichord. She opened the seat and removed a volume of Bach, opened it to the first page of the score and spread it upon the rack. Her hand brushed against the ebony, rested on it lightly, then fingered the catch to open the cover and reveal the two serried rows of manuals. 'I remember that you were always fond of this aria, Ellen,' she said. She sighed gently. 'That Bach loved it, too, is evident in every one of his variations on it. And a famous king had his court musician play it every night to put him to sleep!' She paused, smiling, to consider the ways of kings. Then she asked, hesitantly, 'Will you play it for me, Ellen?'

If she could ever play it right, she could now. And it seemed certain to her that she would as she sat before the ancient instrument, in the famous old room that she had played in so many times before at so many stages of her life. At this moment there was no compulsion; she felt relaxed, settled and sure, at peace. There was no need to look at the score – she knew each note. She did not have to wait for the audience to quiet, nor did she have to make her stage presence known, to put on the mask of her public self. If she wished, she could sit here forever; it was her place and her time. And, as she realized that this was true, Anna Magdalena's aria began to form in her head. The crystalline notes were all there, the space around them existed as it should, the trills were clean and as neat as a frill of lace, a furbelow, the rhythm was vigorous, the cadences precise. She unclasped her hands, edged forward. Her fingers arched, leant to the attack – the keys moved supple beneath her fingers. She had begun, and it was good.

The movement of the sound, the pace and flow of it, mingled with the movements of her hands, the rise and fall of the melody was the rise and fall of her breathing, the music was alive in her, she lived the song. Her being was as firmly rooted in the chords she played, the counter melody in the bass, as her foot on the pedal. There was no division, no disunity; this world she made herself could not be split up into parts: it was one, mighty whole. She was the essence of time itself, she was the motion that carried the stream of tone along; she found herself at the centre of the hard, exact core of each note and on the soft, reverberant edges as well, where sound married sound and new harmony was born.

The past ended before this began and the future did not commence until this was past. This was now,

179

here and undeniable, an eternal instant. Irrevocable, irrefutable, it had a strength and a reality that defied oblivion. With it she was unique, just as it was unique; without it she ceased to exist, just as it was nothing. This power to evoke music depended upon her reading of black marks on a ruled page, upon the dexterity of her fingers and her body's sense of rhythm, upon her knowledge of the way it was, the quality of its sound. But she depended upon it, too, for without it she did not know herself. Outside its orbit she was a bundle of sensations, a walking fear, an appetite, a lawless creature. But when this sound existed, she understood, her life had meaning, order, morality. This was her end, she was its means.

She played the final cadence reluctantly, lifting her hands off the manuals, releasing the mechanism, but holding them barely above it, allowing them to hover, to reconsider, to continue if they wanted. She could go on to the first variation, and the second, and the third – play on until she had gone through all thirty-two of them, and then she could begin again – if she wished. But she did not wish. Her hands fell into her lap and she looked down at them, smiling at her fears of the night past, confident of herself once more. She would not have turned about and looked at Madame Tedescu and asked, 'Did I play well?' – if she had not felt that she must to be polite.

Madame's face was impassive. She seemed not to want to speak. But she did speak, and she spoke quickly, as a doctor gives orders during a critical point in an operation, briskly, with authority. 'You played competently, Ellen. As you say, you have full command of your technique. Your fingers obey your wishes. And as I listened I sensed that you comprehended the music, as a critic comprehends a painting. But a critic cannot paint, a critic is not a musician. What you played was not Bach, Ellen . . .' She stopped. But her glance went on. Her eyes said, You and I know it was once.

She had felt like arguing. Last night – yes, last night had been bad. She would be one of the first to admit that. But today – no, today she had played well. She had heard Bach in her mind, and she had played Bach as she heard it. She could not doubt it. *It had to be.*

But even as she thought this, even as she insisted to herself that Madame was wrong, she had known that Madame was not wrong. She had failed, as she had many times before, but this failure was final. This time she had not known that she had failed – it had sounded right to her. Only through Madame's honesty, at which she railed, had she known.

Madame came over to where she sat by the harpsichord. She carefully closed the covers on the manuals and turned the key in the lock. 'There are many who do not do as well,' she said. 'And they have fame . . . money . . . recognition.'

This was true. She could not even say that her career was over. Jeffry had given her a good notice, Mrs Smythe had approved, her popularity was assured. She could go on playing competently to filled halls, could become a great success and only a few would know there was a difference. But she would not.

'Madame, I do not understand,' she had said. 'It sounded right to me.' She looked up at her old friend hopefully, waited for her to say something more that would make it possible for her to go on. Tell me to practise twenty-four hours a day and I will do it, she thought. Tell me to memorize all of Couperin, go back and study fingering, play Czerny – anything at all if it leaves me a chance to regain what I have lost – and I will do it.

But Madame had only smiled and had shaken her head, had said nothing more. They had talked of other things, inconsequentials, for another quarter of an hour. And then she had left. She had left and come to the park, had bought nuts and sat on the bench, had fed the squirrel until he ran away, until her nuts were gone, and now she was walking again, walking . . . walking.

She was no longer alone. She was walking in a thick crowd of people, mostly women and children, a noisy crowd made up of calls and cries and childish questions, of balloons above and empty boxes of Cracker Jack underfoot. She stopped and looked around her, seeing the people for the first time. This was the zoo, and she was in front of the pony track, obstructing the pushing, pulling file of anxious children who were waiting to ride in the pony-cart. A fat, perspiring, red-faced mother – a captive dirigible of flesh held down by two tugging brats – shouted at her, 'Why don't you move on, lady? You're too old to go on this anyway, and you're only blocking traffic!'

Embarrassed, she did move on, past the man with the tank of helium, who sold balloons, past the snorting seals in their barricaded swimming-pool and up the hill that led to the bear-pits. She did not know where she was going, and she did not care, just so it was to a spot where the crowd was less dense. When, at last, she found herself on a rocky promontory that overhung a den of bears, she decided to stop, to remain there for a while and watch the behaviour of the bears as she had that of the squirrel.

There were two of them out in the warm October sun, big, clumsy, brown bears that lumbered like badly articulated toys as they passed their grotto. She saw that each time they came to the blank cliff face, that formed one wall of their enclosure and above which she was standing, they raised their heads, sometimes sitting upon their haunches, and sniffed her. Then, each time, they resumed their pacing, made the complete circuit of their den, before returning to re-enact this ritual.

The brute power of their huge, mountainous bodies interested her as much as their compulsive actions. Each time they padded towards her, the weight of their strides, the hammer-blows of their feet, shook the rock she stood on, made her own body tremble. They stalked back and forth, around and around the grotto, always together, the larger, darker bear slightly in front of the smaller, rangier one. Each bear's movements were perfectly synchronized with his mate's, except for an occasional corner where the lead bear would be taking shorter, pivotal strides while his companion was still lunging straight ahead. They did not seem to tire, nor did they change their course or in any way modify their actions. And every time they stopped beneath her, looked upwards, sniffing, then sat up, she felt a strange pleasure.

The squirrel had been intelligent, canny, aware of causality and wise in the ways of men; the bears were rigidly conditioned, powerful but unintelligent, automatons. Yet they affected her sensibilities in a manner that the squirrel never could – although she could neither name nor express this reaction, she felt it strongly enough to turn her back upon the enclosure and its two restless occupants, to look the other way towards the city and the sentinel apartment buildings that guarded the periphery of the park.

It seemed to her that she was alienated from her life,

that since her talk with Madame Tedescu she existed outside of all her previous desires and activities, alone and directionless. Even the bears, who still plodded in their pit although she had turned her back on them, were housed; in fact, their quarters determined their lives, condemned them to patrol the unscalable walls of their den, to keep casting their eyes upward at the cliff face and the down-curving, pointed bars that would impale them if they leaped. She was not caged, she was free.

Or so it seemed to her. Basil loved her. Basil did not love her. He was being unfaithful to her with the beautiful girl he had kissed the night before, or he was not being unfaithful to her. Either way it did not seem to matter now.

A great mass of dark clouds were forming behind the high towers of the apartment buildings, making their lineaments stand out in stark relief against the leaden opacity of the approaching storm. In a few minutes the clouds would be over the park and it would begin to rain. She knew that she should begin to walk towards the nearest entrance, if she wanted to avoid a drenching. The atmosphere, which had been warm and damp, had grown cold as she watched the clouds; the breeze had quickened, had blown gusty, and all about her bright red and yellow leaves were flying.

She did not move. A strange calmness had overcome her with her realization that she no longer cared. A tension inside her had been released, an enigmatic, ticking mechanism had ceased to operate, and she now floated in the pool of circumstances that had drowned her desires, was held fast in it, like scum on the surface of a pond. Slowly, lackadaisically, she turned around until she faced the bearpit again. The two brown monsters were coming towards her padding heavily and rhythmically, as if this time they would reach her surely. The larger bear still walked a pace ahead of his mate, still led him, and as she watched, fascinated, she understood just where the resemblance between herself and them lay. But before she could think it through, before the bears could get to the foot of the cliff, the music she had not heard in many months began behind her. A queer, broken humming, an unresonant sound that she could never imitate, a sequence of chords that always seemed about to resolve but never did, this music was the greatest evil she had ever known. Once she had heard it, she could not escape it – she had no control over it – but could only endure it until it lapsed into silence of itself. Yet its evil did not lie in its sound alone, or the terror, the elemental horror, it communicated; the true baseness was *who* accompanied the music. 'I still have time,' she thought, 'to climb that barrier, to throw myself down into the den.' Even as she was thinking this, the discordant humming grew louder and she felt a restraining pressure on her shoulder. She did not have to look to see what it was, she had looked and seen it too many times before; but she did look and saw the hand, the long, white, spatulate fingers, the ring with its deeply-coloured stone that when she gazed into it revealed the night, the swirling blackness, the emptiness of the abyss.

'They are a little like us, aren't they, Ellen?' the sweet voice asked. 'The bears, of course. Look how the old fellow – isn't he tremendous and powerful! – is always in the lead. Now he is sitting up, and in a moment his friend will sit up, too. See, what did I tell you? The second one does exactly what the first one does! Just like you and me, Ellen . . .'

It was Nelle. She did not want to face her. She had hoped she would never see her again. The morning that she had gone up to Dr Danzer's office in the hospital for her last 'treatment' she had said good-bye to Nelle, had told her that she would not recognize her if she came again. And she had thought that Nelle had understood at last. There had been an instant when she lay on the table, while Dr Danzer held her hand and told her that there was no reason to be afraid, that it would all be over in a twinkling, that it was nothing but a shock, an electric shock, that would pass through her frontal lobes, that in some way it would adjust the balance, would make things fit into place again, all things, little and big – there had been this instant, a moment when she first sensed the coldness of the electrodes at her temples, when she had been most terribly afraid despite the warm strength of the doctor's hand, when, ever so faintly, she had heard the humming music, had seen dimly the long, curving fingers, the dark, horrible ring, had known that Nelle was there, too, that she was just lying low, as she always had when Ellen got into trouble, that even after the 'treatment' was over Nelle would not have gone. But this impression had existed for only a moment. Hell had taken its place, white, jumping, searing hell, a blinding, scorching universe of pain. Hours later, when she had recovered consciousness, Nelle was gone. And she had not returned until now.

It would be best to face her, she reasoned – to turn around and look her in the eye and show her that she could not command any more, that she refused to do her bidding. Swiftly, she did turn around, did look Nelle in the face. Nelle had not changed. Nelle still was her twin, her mirror-image. Not that they were the same – they were two different people. Nelle was evil, all evil.

Oh, she could be nice, she could cajole – just look at how she was smiling now, how her eyes were dancing, how her long fingers rested lightly, almost gaily on her own. But she would not stay that way. As soon as she was sure that Ellen would go with her, would do as she told her to, her face would change. Those smiling lips would lengthen into a hag's mouth, those sparkling eyes would begin to glitter with the brightness of malice, those long fingers would bend themselves into claws, and that soft brown hair would coarsen, would grow matted and lack-lustre. And Ellen would have to watch her constantly, would not be able to lose sight of her at any time, would have to fight her when she wanted her to go wrong.

Nelle could not stay. She would not let her. Even if she would have liked to have known where she had been all these months, what she had been doing, she did not dare waste time to talk with her. At once, without considering her for even another minute, she must do the two things Dr Danzer had told her to do if Nelle ever came again. She must tell her what the doctor had said to tell her, and then she must go to the doctor at once. It did not matter what time of the day or night it was, or whether she had an appointment or not, she must go immediately to the doctor. If he were not at his office, she was to tell the nurse to get in touch with him, to get her – or whoever answered the bell – to take her to him or to the nearest hospital. She was to say that it was a matter of life and death. But first, before she went to the doctor, she must do the other thing he had said to do: she must say what he had told her to say to Nelle.

Nelle was still smiling. When she smiled, she was beautiful in a way that Ellen had always wanted to be beautiful. The first time Nelle had come to her – the first time that she could remember; Dr Danzer had said that there must have been other, earlier times, although she did not remember them – she had been looking into the old, cracked mirror above the chiffonier in her father's room. She had run away from the store that afternoon to go with some other girls to a show, and when she got home her father had not let her have any dinner, but had sent her up to his room and told her to lock herself in. This had meant that he was going to come up after dinner and make her take her bloomers off, that he would beat her with his trouser belt until she would not be able to sit down or even lie comfortably – hit her again and again with the long, flailing, snake-like strap, his teeth set in a grimace, his eyes afire. She had hated him, she had wanted to kill him, but she had known that all she could do was what he told her to do. So she had gone upstairs and shut herself, hungry and alone, in his big room with the mahogany bedstead, the picture of Blake's 'Jehovah wrestling with Satan and Adam', the tall chiffonier with the cracked mirror. It had been impossible to sleep, and she had soon grown tired of looking out of the window, so she had gone over to the mirror and she had gazed into it and tried to imagine how her face would be if she were beautiful. That had been the first time she had heard the queer, humming music, too, though then it had not frightened her because she had not known what it meant. She had heard the broken chords and she had felt the hand on her shoulder, had seen Nelle's face in the mirror beside her own. She had thought it was her own face, that it was herself who was humming; but as she had continued to look, as she had heard her father's key turning in the lock of the door, she had realized in panic that it was not her own, that it was altogether different, that

188

it was beautiful. Nelle's voice had sounded in her ear, quiet and sweet, persuading her, 'I'm your friend, Ellen. You can call me Nelle, if you like. I'm here to help you. I know how you can keep your father from hurting you – but you must act quickly! Take your lipstick – yes, your lipstick! Yes, I know he doesn't approve of it, that you always wipe it off before he sees you – but hurry, do as I say before he comes in. I'll explain later. That's it. Rub it all over your mouth, make it red, red and beautiful like mine. Ah, that's fine. Now smile. He has come in the door now, he is standing behind you. Smile, smile dreamily and half close your eyes. Now turn around and put your arms around him. That's it! Hold him to you, harder, harder. Now kiss him. No, not there! On his mouth – his mouth! Ah, that's better.

Her father had torn her arms away from himself, had stared at her, and then had struck her face with the back of his hand. 'You little harlot,' he had whispered. He had picked her up and thrown her on the bed, had whipped her worse than he ever had before. And Nelle had stood there and laughed.

Well, this time she would not get away with it. This time she would not listen to her. She would do just as Dr Danzer had told her to do. Although it was difficult to regard her calmly. Her face was so beautiful, so like, and unlike, her own. It was all she could do to say the words.

'Nelle, you do not exist. I imagine you. You have no life of your own. You cannot make me do anything I do not want to do.' But she had said them, and she had said them loudly and clearly.

Nelle had not gone away, as Dr Danzer had predicted she would. If anything, she had smiled more derisively. 'But haven't you always wanted to do what I told you to do, Ellen? And how can you doubt my existence when you, yourself, see me? It's not as if Dr Danzer had seen me. Of course, he doesn't believe I exist – wouldn't I be foolish to show myself to him?'

'I don't believe you!' Ellen said. And, as she spoke, a raindrop splashed her cheek. It had become darker and darker, until it was all but night in midday. In another few minutes the storm would break. The thing to do was to run. If she ran fast enough she would escape the storm and Nelle. But she must not let her know what she was about to do; she must get as much of a start as possible.

Without looking where she was going, she turned about and began to run. A man and a small boy were coming up the path from the pool of seals, and she blundered into them. The man clutched at her, tried to stop her, cried after her angrily. But she was running in full stride now, her legs striking against the confining hem of her dress. The rain had begun to fall – great wet streaks appeared on the path as she veered past the seals and raced towards the balloon-vendor's stand and the pony-track. Was Nelle behind her? If she turned to see, would she be running after her, gaining on her? It was not worth the chance – she must go faster. Already she was nearly out of breath, and she still had quite a long stretch to go before she reached the entrance to the park. It was raining heavily now, and she could feel the wetness spread along her back, feel the water strike her face. Her legs had begun to ache and each breath she took was painful, but she must go faster yet if she was to be sure to lose Nelle. In another moment or two – three or four at the most – she would reach the exit. A blob of yellow caught her eye, a taxi. It was just pulling up at the traffic light. If she could get there before the light changed, get inside and shut the door – she could tell the taxi-driver to drive off without Nelle. But no matter how much she tried, she did not seem to be able to make her legs move faster. It was like trying to run with two weighty pendulums in place of legs. Each step forward she took she seemed to be lifting a great weight by the tip of her toe. But she was almost there. Another stride . . .

She flung open the door of the taxi, jumped inside and slammed it shut. As she looked forward at the cabby, she saw the light change. 'Get away as fast as you can!' she cried. He glanced at her, nodded his head, and shifted gears. The cab catapulted forward, was half-way down the block before the car that had been beside it was moving. 'Keep on going,' she said. 'I'll tell you where in a moment.'

She had succeeded. But she had not yet gained her breath. It was all she could do to sit back on the seat, to hold on to the strap and look out of the window. The blocks went past, Fifty-ninth, Fifty-eighth, Fifty-seventh, Fifty-sixth. The cab had to stop for another light, but by now she should be safe. She opened her bag and began to look for Dr Danzer's address.

'What are you looking for? May I help you?' The sound of Nelle's sweet voice made her hands go limp. She dropped the bag, let it roll on the floor of the taxi. It was as if she had been dealt a vicious blow in the stomach.

Nelle was sitting in the other corner. She was still smiling, but not breathing heavily, nor was her face flushed, and not a hair of her coiffure was disarranged. 'You didn't think that you could outrun me, did you, Ellen? You know that I could always run faster than you. But, tell me, where are we going? To see Basil?'

She said nothing, but stooped to pick up her bag from the floor. As she reached, the driver swerved the taxi to move into another lane of traffic, and the unexpected jolt made her lose her balance. Clinging to the strap, she leaned forward to get her bag again, but it was not where it had been. Nelle had kicked it into the other corner.

'Why don't you answer me, Ellen?' Nelle had her foot on the open bag. 'I won't let you have this until you tell me. Where are we going?'

There was no reason why she should hide the truth. And there was a good chance that if Nelle discovered that she intended to visit Dr Danzer, Nelle would leave her. At the hospital, when she had been taking her course of shock 'treatments', Nelle had never accompanied her to the doctor. Often she had been waiting for her when she awakened afterwards, but she had not been with her before.

She decided to tell her. 'I am going to see Dr Danzer,' she said. 'He told me to come to him at once if I ever saw you again.'

Nelle's face changed horribly. Her smile was transformed into a sneer, her eyes bulged with anger and her pale skin became suffused with the hot blood of ire. She glared at Ellen hatefully, then bent down and picked up the bag. Snapping it open, she begun to go through it.

Ellen could not let her do this. She threw herself across the seat – on to her enemy – struck out blindly at her face and hands in an attempt to wrest the bag from her. Although she did get her hands on the purse, Nelle proved too strong for her, resisting her as if she were a steel wall, hurting her head, bruising her. In the struggle the bag fell open on the seat and Dr

Danzer's card fell out. Both of them clutched at it, succeeded in touching it. But before either could hold on to it, a sudden gust of wind from the open window sucked at it, made it flutter and fly blindly in a small, dizzy circle like a flame-fascinated moth – while both of them stabbed at it with their hands – then forced it to swoop through the window and into the busy street. As soon as this happened, Nelle relaxed, lay back limply under Ellen's weight. The smile returned to her face – her expression became benign. 'You didn't really want to see the doctor, now did you, Ellen?' she cooed.

Tears of frustration and rage filmed her eyes, and she retreated to her corner of the cab, weak with exasperation. The taxi had halted at another light, and she could see the cabby's face in the rear-view mirror, his eyes dull with bewilderment.

'Are you all right, lady?' he asked. And when Ellen did not, at first, answer, he asked again, 'Are you sure you're all right, lady? You aren't sick or nothing?'

Nelle was signalling to her to answer, to say something sensible.

'I'm quite all right, thank you,' she said. 'Just feeling a little tired.'

'I heard a commotion back there,' the cabby said, turning around and peering at Nelle's corner. 'I heard you talking pretty loud, as if somebody else was there. Have you decided where you're going?'

'I think we'll go home,' Nelle answered sweetly, before Ellen could speak, before she had decided what to say or whether to say anything at all. 'We're a little tired and wet.' And she gave the driver Ellen's home address.

'I don't know why you wanted to see that foolish doctor,' she complained to Ellen. 'He's not your friend,

193

as I am. He would only make you go back to the hospital and take another course of "treatments". I'd rather see Basil. I always liked Basil – I think he's handsome, you know – and I haven't seen him in so long a time!'

Ellen did not answer her. She sat very still in her own corner, holding her aching head, her eyes shut. If she were silent, if she said nothing, Nelle might get bored and go away. But if she did not choose to, Ellen knew from long experience that there was no way she could make her go. She felt sick and weak, frightened, alone . . .

Nelle kept on talking, softly, quietly, but with a deliberate vehemence. 'Dr Danzer has never understood you or me,' she said, 'for all his big words and fancy ideas. He hasn't helped you either. You are just the same as you always were, Ellen – a silly little wretch who is afraid of her own shadow when I'm not there! But I'm always there, Ellen, when you need me, whether you admit it or not, whether you choose to remember me later or not. I was there when you were a girl and your father whipped you – if it hadn't been for me you would never have stood up to him, never been allowed to go out alone or with your friends, never been permitted to go away to the conservatory. And I was there, too, that night when you walked the streets alone and the men mocked you, when you went up to your hotel room to wait for Jim to come back to you, meekly, humbly, ready to forgive him if he only returned! If it hadn't been for me you would have forgiven him, wouldn't you? Yet what thanks do I get? You won't even remember what I did – you let that doctor of yours with his psychiatric mumbo-jumbo persuade you that it never happened, you let him convince you that I did not try to kill Jim that night, that the little you do remember of what happened

194

was only an expression of the guilt you're supposed to feel towards your father!'

Ellen turned away from her and her diabolical words. Gazing out the window at the brownstone fronts, the tenements, the pillars of the Third Avenue 'El', she could almost succeed in not hearing the softly spoken statements, the terrible lies – or truths? – with which Nelle tormented her. But her indifference did not discourage Nelle. She kept on with her spate of accusations, her taunts and her boasting.

'What happened when you told Dr Danzer about me? Tell me, what happened?' she cajoled. But when Ellen refused to answer, she supplied the response herself. 'He told you that I was only a figment of your imagination, didn't he? He said that you had withdrawn from reality – what a catch-phrase that is! – when you found the life you led too unpleasant, too frustrating, and had invented me to be your companion. Do you believe that, Ellen? Do you believe that you invented me? Rather that I invented you, I who am your better part! You can't live without me, Ellen, and you know it.

'What else did that doctor of yours say about me? Oh, yes, the funniest thing of all! Do you remember how we laughed about it at the time, Ellen? When he told you that the best proof you could have that I did not exist – as if you could ever prove that I did not exist, I who am more real than you are yourself – was the fact that my name was your own spelled backwards, do you remember how we laughed, how we rolled on the floor and laughed when he told you that? And do you remember that last concert of yours before you went to the hospital, that concert when you were so frightened and your fingers would not obey you, when I had to play instead of you, when we exchanged roles and you stood beside me and I played? What would you have done without me then, Ellen? Would you have just sat there before your instrument, with the entire concert hall filled with people who had come to hear you play, and have stared at the manuals unable to lift a finger, terrified because you could not hear the music in your head? Yes, that is what you would have done – ah, I know you! – if I had not taken your place, if I had not played for you!'

Ellen let her rave on. Part of what she said was true, but the greater part of it was subtly distorted. At her last concert before she had become ill and Basil had taken her to Dr Danzer, she had forgotten what she was to play, she had not been able to hear the notes sound in her head as she always had before. But she had played – she herself had played and no one else. This much she knew. This much she must hold on to. It had come out wrong, everything had got all jumbled up, her hands had roved the manuals like wild distrait creatures – but she had played, not Nelle. It had been Nelle who had stood behind her, who had mocked and laughed at her, who had tried her best to distract her. And it had been Nelle who had run forward across the stage when she could not play any longer, when the effort to control her wild hands had become too much for her, who had lunged across the footlights at the great, many-faced beast she hated, who had thrown herself screaming upon them, cursing them, reviling them. It had been Nelle, not Ellen.

The taxi parked in front of her house, and Ellen, who had recaptured her purse after the doctor's card had been lost, paid the driver. As she opened the door, Nelle, rudely, squeezed past her and rushed up the steps to the door of her house before she could step to the street. While she fitted her key in the lock, Nelle stood beside her, breathing violently, her lips open passionately, her hands warm and feverish on her shoulder. 'Tell me about Basil, Ellen,' she kept saying. 'Tell me all about him. Is he still as tall, as lean and blond as he was? I can hardly wait to see him!'

She had anticipated a struggle with her when she opened the door, since she had decided that whatever happened she would not let Nelle see Basil first. But as the door opened they both stood motionless in surprise. The hall was filled with the full, sweet tones of a violin. And as they listened, the sound stopped, broke off in the midst of a passage, as it might if someone had pulled back on the hand that held the bow.

Nelle led Ellen into the hall of her own house, led her on tip-toe to the library door. Together, they stood behind it while Nelle pushed it open a crack, far enough to see into the big, book-lined room.

Basil was standing by the piano, his arms around a woman. The violin had been laid aside on the piano bench, forgotten. He held her passionately, and her long auburn hair had come undone, falling in profusion along his shoulders as soft, coppery dusk sometimes falls upon the hills and the sea.

Then Nelle closed the door and turned to Ellen, smiling. 'You see,' she said, 'I am your only friend.'

7

'I am your only friend.' Nelle was present in the darkness, in the foul, seething blackness – Nelle was close to her, bending over her as she lay stiff and tense beneath the bed-clothes, Nelle's sweet whisper echoing in the silence of the room. She had come to expect Nelle's appearance at this point of her compulsive journey into the past, had come to accept it and to make no attempt to fight it off, although she knew that it meant that the greatest terror of all was coming, would be upon her before the night was done. Nelle's hand touched her now, the long fingers grew dimly before her eyes, strips of shadow only slightly lighter than the surrounding, threatening darkness. Against them, slowly, she saw vertical bars – the fingers seemed to rest against the bars, but on the other side of them. Then, as on the other nights, the ring on the longest of the fingers took shape, the horrible stones in its centre flickered and came alive, became a deepness, a soul-sucking vacuum towards which she herself was drawn, upon which her consciousness was focused, into which, inevitably, she must go. She felt herself contracting, growing smaller and smaller, and at the same time moving up towards the bars, the dark aperture of the stone, being pulled into it as thread is pulled into the eye of a needle.

She resisted this magnetism, knowing that she could not resist it long enough. By compressing herself until her bones ached and her skin was taut with the straining of her muscles, she managed to achieve an equilibrium, a delicate poise, on the threshold of the dark entrance within the ring. And it was at this moment that she seemed to stop existing. As she hesitated, by means of an ultimate exertion of will, on the rim of nothingness, the present instant stood still, Nelle's sweet, coaxing voice froze in mid-syllable, her future came rushing towards her, bringing with it a tremendous impact of experience – as if all the events that were to happen had been poured into a funnel and she was at the bottom of the spout – and her past overtook her, swelled up and around her, spread out on all sides.

A nest of bars, a menagerie of vertical and horizontal lines, cage upon cage upon cage, and she herself in the centre of them all – no matter where she cast her gaze, she saw bars, some round and ivoried white, some square and darkly painted and curving downward to end in points, some themselves shadows on the face of a sleeping man (two sets of these, one seen in the silver light of the moon, the other redly in the glare of a neon sign), and a final set – the closest, the most threatening of all – which seemed to press against her temples as if she were peering through them, on the other side of which the vague, dark shapes of the elms could hardly be seen.

Nelle's voice began again, time began again; but the vision of the world of bars did not disappear. Nelle was saying, 'This is you, Ellen. Believe it if you can – for this is what Dr Danzer says – these bars are you. These are the bars of your crib as a child, the bars you saw in the park that were meant to protect you from the den of bears, the bars of shadow cast by two, different blinds at two, different hotel windows on two, different nights upon Jim Shad's face, and the bars on the window of this room, the latticework that casts the checkered pattern on the floor. These bars, so the doctor says, are your fate – you can't escape them, although you can learn to prevail over them by making the best of them, as a caged creature rubs against the bars of its enclosure. Look at them, Ellen; see how they confine you, how they warp and twist your actions, how they influence your thoughts, how they make you.'

A great chill settled upon her – the coldness of the irrevocable – and the fear she had known long enough to grow accustomed to grew in intensity until it regained its pristine force: the terror of a child. She realized that she had been thrown back in time to an unknown period of her childhood, that she was small and bewildered, awakened out of sleep to stare at the darkness, to listen again for the unexplained sound she had heard in her crib. Suddenly the sound came again: a creaking of the stairs, a giggling, her mother's voice protesting, 'But I'll have to look in at the child; she may not be asleep.' Then, a loud noise and a bright streak of light appeared out of which two monstrous forms, two genii as in the fairy-tales, burgeoned and approached her crib. They stood over her, blocking the light, laughing and struggling, bending down to get her. *'Don't you do it!* I tell you she is too young to touch any of that!' More struggling above her. More menacing shadows that grew and wavered and swooped down on her. An hysterical giggle, a high screaming, 'Don't! Don't!

Oh, you're terrible!' Again the larger shadow bending over her, coming nearer and nearer, and with it a queer stench. The lights suddenly brighter, blinding her, the hand – her mother's hand with its queer dark stone – upon the bars of her crib, the great fear looming out of her and the great hate – the huge, senseless force of hate that she had never felt before streaming out of her, directed towards the shadow, as her mother cried again, *'If you touch a hair of her head, I'll murder you!'*

The shadows came down upon her, blanketing her, but the terror subsided; she felt herself grow again, move forward in time, move out of the small world of a child into the larger, more complex environment of an adult. The darkness still surrounded her, yet now it was the natural darkness of night. The air was cool on her brow and she lay back peacefully on Basil's arm, her head resting upon his shoulder, as the carriage they were riding in moved slowly through the park. About them the scent of freshly drenched verdure pervaded the atmosphere – the storm had passed and the vaulted firmament above them was brightened with the flashings of a thousand stars. Nelle sat across from them, sulking. For Ellen had not looked at her in many hours, and was now sure that eventually she would become tired of her game and leave them to themselves.

Basil's hand had held her own, Basil's rangy form rested beside hers; she felt almost secure and safe. The long afternoon she had passed shut up in her own room listening to the intermittent sounds of the violin belonged to the past. Throughout the afternoon Nelle had tried again and again to force Ellen to go down to the library and confront the lovers. If she had steadfastly refused to do this, it had not been out of any confidence that her impression was mistaken, or out of dread that her worst suspicions would be verified. Instead, she had sat and looked at a picture on the wall, a print of Picasso's that she particularly liked, had focused all her thoughts upon its form and shape, had studied it as if she were seeing it for the first time. Nelle had kept pacing back and forth across the floor, her smile turned to a scowl, berating her, pretending at times that she could see into the room downstairs, could watch its occupants and describe their love-making to Ellen. She had refused to listen, and had at last reduced Nelle to sullen silence and an even more frenetic pacing.

At the end of the afternoon the violin's sound ceased altogether. The door to the library was heard opening, and the high, musical voice of a woman penetrated to her room. Nelle, gnashing her teeth, flung herself upon Ellen, pulled at her, cursed her, in a final attempt to get her to go out in the hall and interrupt the meeting. But Ellen had shut her eyes and withstood her urgings. When she had looked through the narrow crack of the door and had seen the auburn-haired girl in Basil's arms, the calmness of certainty had descended upon her. She knew then that her husband's infidelity was a fact – from that moment on anything else she might have learned would only have been a detail. Not that it had been possible at all times in the afternoon to suppress her imagination: occasionally the sound of laughter had been heard, of talk and – once – the sound of something falling. But if she had followed Nelle's promptings and had broken in on them, she would only have been adding to her own jealousy.

A little later, after she was certain that Basil's visitor had gone, she went down to the library. Nelle had stayed behind her all the way down the stairs, had walked into the room with her and had seated herself

203

in one of the wingback chairs by the fireplace where she would be best able to see what occurred. Basil had been seated at his desk, but had looked up when he saw Ellen approaching. He had come to her and taken her in his arms and had kissed her complacently on the brow. She had let him do this because she had not felt deeply about it. He was her husband, she was his wife, he was unfaithful to her. The three facts, despite their seeming relevance to each other, had been kept separate and unconnected in her mind. What was happening and how she acted seemed to her to be unimportant, distant matters that were curious to observe and even debatable, but not in actuality a part of her life. Nelle, who sat on the other side of them, sneering at them, was real, her hatred of Basil – which was the greater because of her recent passion – was incontestable, and Ellen felt it as she might feel the warmth of a great fire even at some distance. But Nelle was also not a part of her.

They had gone out to dinner, and had sat and talked afterwards over their coffee. Nelle had accompanied them, had remained near them, watching them. Most of the time Ellen had managed to ignore her unwavering, insolent stare, but she had not been able to forget that it was on her. Nelle's presence had fitted into the back of her mind and nagged her like a worry. It was in the hope that a drive in the park might serve to vanquish Nelle that she had suggested to Basil that they hire a carriage after leaving the restaurant. Nelle had not left them as they entered the park, but she had seemed to grow less oppressive, and Ellen sensed that she would soon give up and go in the face of their felicity. Nelle depended on violence, on frustration, on hate.

The carriage slipped smoothly forward along the wide road, the horse's hooves slopping placidly and the driver's cocked hat bobbing irregularly as he smoked his pipe. Nelle had been looking at them intently ever since they had entered the carriage, but now she looked away. Ellen sighed and allowed herself to relax even more. Nothing was right, she realized, but life went on, jogged slowly past each day in much the same way the carriage moved gradually past each dark clump of trees. The trick was to learn to be indifferent.

Then Basil cleared his throat and sat up. He had looked thin and restless in the reflected light of the street lamps, and vaguely unhappy.

'Ellen,' he had said, 'there is something I would like to talk to you about.'

She had looked at him and nodded her head, had waited for him to continue. But he had hesitated, had fumbled in his pocket for a cigarette and had taken a long time lighting it before he spoke again. 'It's about your concert, Ellen. Last night's concert, I mean. I'm not sure you should give another one.'

She had not expected this. Her face stiffened and, although she knew it was the last thing she should do, she had looked across at Nelle. She did not look back at Basil. Nelle had held her hand up so that the ring with its dark stone had caught the dim light of the lamps. Its deeps of darkness had their old effect on her: she felt herself drawn irresistibly towards its horrible emptiness. Nelle had begun to smile and to gain substance and distinctness – Ellen felt as if she were flowing towards her, even though she knew that she had not moved. She tried to take her eyes off the ring, but it was impossible.

'Why are you sitting over there now?' Basil asked. 'I had no intention of insulting you. I said what I did for your own good.' Ellen was startled to see that Basil was looking past her and speaking to Nelle, that Nelle was no longer gazing at her, but at Basil.

'I am not over there. I'm here beside you,' she said. Yet before she had stopped speaking, she had glanced down at where her own body should be, and realized that she could not see herself. Nelle, however, was frighteningly visible.

Basil paid no attention to what she said. He continued to look at Nelle – whose eyes were glinting wildly and whose hair had become disarrayed. 'I went to see Dr Danzer today,' he went on. 'I told him that you had – had difficulties last night. I asked him what was wrong.'

Nelle laughed scornfully. 'You poor fool! I suppose you believed what he told you?' she said.

Basil shook his head worriedly, stubbed out his cigarette and threw it away. 'Don't listen to her, Basil. Please, don't listen to her,' Ellen cried.

But Basil did not seem to hear her. He went over to the other side of the carriage and sat beside Nelle. When he attempted to put his arm around her, she shrank away and clawed at his face.

'Darling, you're ill!' he said. 'You've worked too hard too soon, and now you're on the verge of another breakdown. You must listen to me!' (Nelle was laughing again, showing her teeth.) 'Dr Danzer is quite concerned. He wants to see you, to talk to you. He says it is not at all unusual for a musician, after a course of shock "treatments", to experience difficulty in regaining his previous skills. He thinks that you may well be ill again, that you may need more "treatments".'

Nelle struck his face with her open hand, her nails digging into his cheek's flesh, gouging it, leaving long, deep scratches from which the blood flowed freely. 'Didn't the doctor tell you that might happen when you gave your consent for the "treatments"?' she demanded. 'Didn't he tell you that an artist's skill is lost when that current passes through the brain – that if an adjustment is made later it will be on a lower level?' She stood up in the gently swaying carriage and pointed her long finger at him accusingly. Her face was a mask of hate. Ellen shrank from the sight.

Basil's hand rubbed at his bleeding cheek. 'The doctor told me that,' he said. 'He also told me that your chance to recover was slight without the shock "treatment". I had to make a decision.'

Nelle spat at him, then jumped from the slowly moving carriage. Her hair streaming in wild disorder down her back, she ran swiftly across the road to the path that led to the zoo. Basil jumped out and ran after her, crying, 'Ellen! Ellen! Stop and listen to what I have to say!'

The driver pulled on the reins and halted the carriage. Ellen leaped out, too, and began to run after both of them down the curving path. Basil was a good way ahead of her, and Nelle was almost out of sight; in her desperate hurry to catch up with them, to stop what she felt was about to happen, she deserted the twisting walk and ran down the hill, through brambles and against low branches of trees that she could not see in the night. Nelle, she knew, was running towards the bear-pit.

Ellen got there in time to see Nelle, who had fallen in her headlong flight and whose clothes were torn to ribbons, climbing the bars that overhung the grotto. The creatures below were moving about restlessly; one of them was growling. By the time Nelle had reached the top of the bars, was outlined whitely against the dark iron rods, Basil had begun to climb after her.

'Don't do it, Basil!' Ellen cried. 'Leave her alone – let her do whatever she wants. She is not me! I am here!'

But if Basil had heard, he had given no indication. He had kept on climbing up the bars, holding on with one hand and his twining legs as he reached out for Nelle with the other. She was perched on the outermost limit of the barrier, clinging carelessly to the arching points of the bars. Beneath her the bears, huge, lumbering shadows in the night, padded heavily, sniffing and growling. Then Nelle had started to teeter, to swing back and forth as if she were losing her balance, and Basil redoubled his effort to get to her in time.

Ellen watched helplessly. There had been nothing she could do. Each time she called out to her husband he ignored her – he seemed only to have ears for the blasphemous taunts Nelle threw at him. But as Ellen, her hands clenching and unclenching, had watched the perilous climb, she had remembered a similar experience – a horrifying time – not too long ago. She had remembered awaking in a hotel room with Jim Shad lying beside her. A neon sign blinked on and off outside the window, casting a pattern of red and black bars across his sleeping face. She had left the bed to walk to the window and change the angle of the slats so that the light did not fall on his face, when she felt the familiar pressure on her shoulder, had turned and had looked into Nelle's face. That time she had screamed, and the scream had awakened Jim. He had jumped up and run – not to her, but to Nelle. She had hit him again and again with the heavy base of a lamp, and had beaten him until he had fallen back gasping on the bed. Then she had begun to batter his head against the bedpost, while Ellen watched and screamed her terror.

This time she knew it was useless to cry out. She could not have even if she had wanted to, for Basil had reached the top, the outermost bars, and was working his way laboriously across their points towards Nelle. To scream would have been to startle him, perhaps to cause him to lose his balance and plunge into the pit. Ellen could only stand by and wait.

But Nelle had screamed. Just as Basil had been reaching her, she had begun to shriek – great, full-throated cries. Basil had thrown out his hands in an attempt to save himself, but he had already lost his equilibrium. As he pitched downwards, he caught at the point of a bar with one hand; she saw the flesh torn by the cruel edge. Then his body dropped into the pit with a heavy thud, the cumbersome shadows moved in, and he cried out piteously. Nelle had climbed down as soon as he fell and had run to Ellen, had put her hand over Ellen's mouth and held tightly on to her to keep her from running for help until it was too late and the only sounds that came from the bear-pit were hideously inhuman.

The room was dark, the darkness settled all around her, seething and twisting, claiming her for its own. Even the window was dark now, the moon having passed behind a cloud. She had lived through it for another night and had witnessed it all once again, helpless to intervene. Any time she closed her eyes, day or night, it was likely to begin again; but she did not have to close her eyes to hear those screams. Their piercing ululation filled her ears whether she waked or slept, banishing music forever, creating their own symphony of pain. And another sound was at all times with her: a sweet, lying whisper, advising, cajoling, misleading her. Nelle rarely left her now, seeming almost a part of her, spoke for her, acted for her, often even forced her to think her thoughts. Sometimes it seemed that she was not Ellen, that she was Nelle.

CANONGATE CRIME CLASSICS

 Bringing you some of the most exciting and chilling crime novels of the last sixty years in an accessible, mass-market format.

The Deadly Percheron

John Franklin Bardin

"Bardin was ahead of his time . . . there is a visionary lucidity about Bardin's nightmares that makes his surrealist logic both convincing and disturbing."   Julian Symons

1 84195 013 0

£5.99 pbk

Devil Take the Blue-Tail Fly

John Franklin Bardin

"The reader of these tales will read in horror – those who can take it. And they will not forget very soon."
Patricia Highsmith

1 84195 164 1

£5.99 pbk

A Rage in Harlem

Chester Himes

"A crime writer of Chandlerian subtlety though in a vein of sheer toughness very much his own."   The Times

1 84195 024 6

£5.99 pbk

Cotton Comes to Harlem

Chester Himes

"Chester Himes is perhaps the most singular American novelist of the past century, whose insight and innovation are still only beginning to be recognised." The Independent

1 84195 161 7

£5.99 pbk

The Chill

Ross Macdonald

"The finest series of detective novels ever written by an American." William Goldman, The New York Times

1 84195 118 8

£5.99 pbk

The Drowning Pool

Ross Macdonald

"Ross Macdonald remains the grand-master, taking the crime novel to new heights by imbuing it with psychological resonance, complexity of story, and richness of style that remain awe-inspiring." Jonathan Kellerman

1 84195 117 X

£5.99 pbk

I Spit on Your Graves

Boris Vian

"Vian is a great writer, absolutely one of a kind, full of pain and the presence of death but full, too, of joy and play, long unknown to English-language readers." James Sallis

1 84195 104 8

£5.99 pbk

The Shark-Infested Custard

Charles Willeford

"No one writes a better crime novel than Charles Willeford." Elmore Leonard

1 84195 026 2

£5.99 pbk

CANONGATE CRIME

 An innovative list that brings together outstanding crime writers from around the world.

Bone in the Throat

Anthony Bourdain

"Sharper than the doper chef's $450 customized Japanese carving knife . . . Satirical and prodigiously self-assured." New York Times Book Review

1 84195 096 3

£5.99 pbk

Gone Bamboo

Anthony Bourdain

"Following his hilarious first novel, *Bone in the Throat*, with another antic tale, Bourdain establishes himself as the new master of the wiseass crime comedy." Publishers Weekly

0 86241 825 9

£10.00 pbk

Deadman

Jon A. Jackson

"How long can Jon A. Jackson remain the best-kept secret

of hard-boiled crime fiction connoisseurs?" New York Times
1 84195 057 2
£10.00 pbk

Dead Folks

Jon A. Jackson
"*Dead Folks* reads like an episode of *The Fugitive* written by a clever if slightly dishevelled Elmore Leonard . . . Jackson's inventiveness never falters" The Washington Post
1 84195 103 X
£9.99 pbk

Hit on the House

Jon A. Jackson
"For once comparisons are merited: mention of Jon A. Jackson in the same sentence as the late Charles Willeford is deserved." The Guardian
1 84195 102 1
£5.99 pbk

Blue Lonesome

Bill Pronzini
"There is a sharp sense of place in this moody crime novel, which evokes even the inner landscape of the hero's mind. For all the spareness of the style, this is a rich study of alienated people and the big open spaces where they live." The New York Times Book Review
1 84195 130 7
£9.99 pbk

Shirker

Chad Taylor
"Reminiscent of Paul Auster's *New York Trilogy* and with

peripheral detail as obsessive as Easton Ellis's *American Psycho*." The Times
1 84195 119 6
£5.99 pbk

Safe House

Andrew Vachss

"Andrew Vachss' work is all about horror, outrage, moral indignation and the blood of commitment. Vachss is the voice of righteousness confronting a powerful and cowardly evil." James Ellroy
1 84195 108 0
£5.99 pbk

Run

Douglas E. Winter

"*Run* doesn't run, it flies. The style is terrific. What Winter does here is open a new school: how to write thrillers with a pace that takes your breath away." Elmore Leonard
1 84195 100 5
£5.99 pbk

You can order direct from:

Canongate Books Ltd
14 High Street
Edinburgh EH1 1TE
Tel (0131) 557 5111
Fax (0131) 557 5211

www.canongate.net